John Codman

Winter Sketches from the Saddle

John Codman

Winter Sketches from the Saddle

ISBN/EAN: 9783337252618

Printed in Europe, USA, Canada, Australia, Japan

Cover: Foto ©Andreas Hilbeck / pixelio.de

More available books at **www.hansebooks.com**

FROM THE SADDLE

BY A SEPTUAGENARIAN

———

JOHN CODMAN

———

NEW YORK AND LONDON

G. P. PUTNAM'S SONS

The Knickerbocker Press

TO

GEORGE BANCROFT,
THE OCTOGENARIAN EQUESTRIAN,
THE HISTORIAN FOR ALL TIME,
THIS VOLUME
IS BY PERMISSION
RESPECTFULLY DEDICATED.

WINTER SKETCHES.

CHAPTER I.

Equestrianopathy.—The Horse, the Saddle, and the Outfit.—Westchester County.—Elephants and Milk.—Decker's Institution.— A Town of Churches.—Meeting of Old Schoolmates.

I HAVE a favorite medical system, which I shall style Equestrianopathy. It is vastly superior to Allopathy, Homœopathy, Electropathy or pathy of any other kind.

"When pain and anguish wring the brow," whether it comes from mental or physical depression, too much exercise of brain or stomach, dissipation of society or confinement in furnace-heated hotels or offices of the city, I resort to my remedy.

From my boyhood I have adopted it whenever opportunity offered, as a prophylactic as well as a cure. Many hundred miles have I ridden over African deserts, South American pampas and the plains and mountains of California, Utah and Idaho; and the miles traversed in New York and New England might be counted by thousands. But for the horse I should long ago have been in the grave.

"My kingdom for a horse!" exclaimed Richard. The horse has been a kingdom for me.

I could say with Campbell

"Cease every joy to glimmer on my mind,
But leave, oh leave the light of hope behind,"

that light of hope being my saddle horse.

The late Rev. Dr. Cutler of Brooklyn, when a feeble young man recovered his health by riding from Portland to Savannah. His valuable life was prolonged to old age by this almost daily exercise. When one of his parishioners asked him how he could afford to keep a horse, his reply was "My dear sir, I cannot afford not to keep one."

If your business confines you to the city, give the night two hours that you now steal from it, and take for the day two hours that you give for sleep. Take this clear gain of time for horseback exercise in the park.

But if you are a man of leisure, ride through the country for days and weeks on long journeys, where constantly recurring changes divert the mind that stagnates in daily routine.

Procure—I mean buy, own, an animal that is exclusively a saddle horse. A horse is like a servant in one especial respect, "A servant of all work" is perfect in nothing. She is a poor cook, a poor parlor-girl and a poor chambermaid. A horse that goes double and single in harness and is likewise used under the saddle, walks, trots and lopes indifferently. A good driving and riding horse is a rare combination, and a horse generally used in harness is never capable of any prolonged journey under the saddle.

Select a horse whose weight corresponds in proportion to your own. He should be a fast walker, a good trotter and an easy loper. A fast walk is the quality most desirable though not often sufficiently considered. Walk your horse half the time and divide the other half between the trot and the lope. Now as to the saddle. The little "pig skin" is adapted to hunting and is well enough for play and exercise in the park. It is used by exquisites who ape all things English. Did you ever notice that such persons invariably carry a Malacca joint with a rectangular ivory or steel handle, a loop at the other end of the stick? Ask them the use of it and they will tell you that it is the fashion.

Really it is useful to country gentlemen of England, who, riding where lanes and gates abound, are enabled without dismounting, to catch the gate latch, and to close the gate after them with the handle. They also put a lash into the loop when hunting, but the thing is a useless encumbrance here.

The English saddle is not well adapted to long journeys. It often galls the horse's back, which the unstuffed Mexican or McClellan never does, if properly put on far enough aft and with a blanket underneath.

Especially is this true in regard to a lady's saddle. If a horse could speak he would tell you which he likes best. I wish that Balaam's ass when he was in a conversational mood, had said something definite on the subject of saddles. Be kind, while you are firm with your horse. Don't carry a whip—he will see it and suspect you. Wear light spurs, which are good persuasives and which he will think have touched him accidentally, while at the same time they serve to keep him awake.

Loosen the girths frequently when you alight, and when you stop for any time remove the saddle and wash his back. The beast will thank you with his grateful eyes.

Do not give him water when hot, excepting enough to wet his mouth. Feed him when cool, but feed neither him nor yourself immediately before starting, nor when greatly fatigued. The neglect of this precaution may induce dyspepsia for a horse as well as for a man. I am writing for people upon whom this treatment is urged that they may avoid or be cured of that distressing malady. It is old as the world. It came from the indigestible apples of the Garden of Eden.

Virgil thus describes it:

> "—rostroque immanis vultur obunco
> Immortale jecur tondens fecundaque poenis
> Viscera rimaturque epulis, habitatque sub alto
> Pectore, nec fibris requies datur ulla renatis."

That is a vivid description of dyspepsia. It is what the priestess thought as worth her while to take Aeneas down to hell to behold, that among other terrible sights he might see poor Tityus in one of its fits.

Don't trust the most honest face in the world in the matter of oats. See them put into the manger, and hang about the stable until your horse is fed. Get your own dinner afterwards, for you are of less importance. If your table is not properly served you can complain. Your horse cannot. Do not overload him with much baggage. Dead weight tells upon him more that live weight. Dismount occasionally when about to descend a long or steep hill. You will thus relieve the horse and vary the exercise of your own muscles. Wear a woollen shirt and let him carry your night-shirt, hair-brush, tooth-brush, bathing sponge, a few collars and handkerchiefs ; they will weigh but little over two pounds and will be all sufficient.

Feed your horse with four quarts of oats in the morning, two at noon and six at night, and with all the hay that he cares to eat.

Now let us start on a short ride of twenty-eight miles and return.

It is the middle of November, in a season when the autumn has prematurely succumbed to the frosts of winter, and the scene of our departure is at Lake Mohegan, one of those beautiful and romantic basins among the hills

of Westchester County which divides its attractions with its neighbors, Mahopac, Oscawana,
Mohansic and Osceola, all of them within fifty
miles of New York, and all, with the exception
of Mahopac, little known and almost undis-
turbed in the seclusion of nature. The people
of the crowded city who go out of it in the summer to the Kaaterskills, the White Mountains or
to the greater altitudes in more distant Colora-
do, surely have not informed themselves of the
scarcely less romantic scenery and healthful climate that is within their reach in an hour. Here
in the hills, which almost deserve the name of
mountains, are primeval forests and leafy sol-
itudes, rushing torrents and quiet glens that need
no distance to lend enchantment to the view.
Most of this soil is too rough for remunerative
agriculture, and it is difficult to understand how,
with all their industry and economy, the hardy
inhabitants manage to gain a livelihood.

The roads were hard and smooth and the clatter of my horse's hoofs rang cheerily in the crisp
air when I left Mohegan. A lively gallop soon
brought us fourteen miles on our way easterly
over the hills to the little village of Somerstown.
Like a great castle on the Rhine, with its
two or three adjacent appurtenances, a large

brick hotel looms up among the few small
houses in its neighborhood. My curiosity was
not only attracted by this disproportion, but by
the statue of an elephant nearly as large as life ;
I mean the life size of a small elephant, of
course.

This remarkable resemblance to the animal
was mounted on a high post before the door
of the hotel, and painted over the front of the
building I read, in enormous letters, " Elephant
Hotel."

It was time to breathe my horse, and the
ride had given me an appetite for any thing I
might find within, even if it should prove to
be an elephant steak. The landlord observed
that "the women-folks were not at home, but
he guessed he could find something." He accordingly placed a cold turkey and a bottle of
London porter on the table, and thus proved
that his guess was very correct. As he sat
down by my side, I asked him the meaning of
all this elephantine display.

"Why," he answered, "Hackaliah Bayley
built this house himself!"

" Hackaliah Bayley ! Who was he ? "

" Who was Hackaliah Bayley ! Don't you
know? He was the man who imported the

first elephant into these U-nited States—old Bet; of course you have heard of old Bet?"

"No, I have not."

"What, never heard of old Bet! Well, sir, you are pretty well along in life. Where have you been all your days?"

I told him I had not spent them all in West-chester County.

"I should rather think not," replied the land-lord, "or else you'd have heard of Hackaliah Bayley and old Bet. Right here, from this very spot, he started the first show in this country. Right around here is where they breed and winter wild animals to this day. Folks round here have grown rich out of the show business. There's men in this town that have been to Asia and Africa to get animals; and Bayley's big circus (he was old Hackaliah's son) grew up out from the small beginning when Hackaliah imported old Bet, and that wasn't more than sixty or seventy years ago. Yes, sir; Hackaliah began on that one she-elephant. He and a boy were all the company. They travelled nights and showed daytimes. Old Bet—she knew just how much every bridge in the country would bear before she put her foot on it. Bimeby they got a cage of monkeys

and carted them along, and gradually it got up
to bears, lions, tigers, camels, boa-constrictors,
alligators, Tom Thumb, hippopotamuses, and
the fat woman—in fact, to where it is now.
Yes, sir ; P. T. Barnum got the first rudiments
of his education from Hackaliah Bayley right
here in Somerstown. Elephants and milk have
made this town. In fact, we all live on elephants and milk."

" Elephants and milk ! Good gracious, " I
exclaimed, "what a diet ! "

" Lord, sir, " retorted my landlord, "did
you think I meant that we crumbled elephants
into milk and ate 'em ? No ; I mean to say
that the elephant business and the milk business are what have built up this place. I've
told you what elephants have done for us, and
now I'll tell you about milk. There's farmers
round here owning a hundred cows apiece.
From the little depot of Purdy's you'll pass a
mile beyond this, we send eight thousand
gallons of milk every day to New York : and it
starts from here pure, let me tell you, for we
are honest, if we were brought up in the show
business. Then right in our neighborhood are
two condensed-milk factories, where they use
seventeen thousand more. There's twenty-

five thousand gallons. The farmers get twelve cents for it on the spot. So you see there is a revenue of three thousand dollars a day to this district. Now you've been telling me of the West, how they raise forty bushels of wheat to the acre, and all that. Well, what does it amount to by the time they get their returns, paying so much out in railroad freight? You ride along this afternoon, and if you come back this way, tell me if the houses and fixings and things, especially the boys, and more particularly the gals, look any better in them fever-and-ague diggings than they do here, if we do live on elephants and milk!"

And so I parted from Mr. Mead, with many thanks for the valuable information I should never have been likely to acquire by travelling on a railroad.

I soon came to Purdy's station, and dismounting at the door of the factory was politely shown the various processes by which the raw material of cow product is manufactured and reduced. One gallon of pure milk is reduced to half a pint of the condensed, and to this sugar is added for long preservation, although it is not required if the milk is to be used in two or three weeks. There is perhaps

a greater assurance of purity in the new stock
than in the old stock, which is liable to be
watered; still it might be readily imagined
that arrowroot and other ingredients may
form a basis for deception if the known integrity of those who manufacture it, did not
place them above suspicion.

As I jogged along upon my road I overtook
a gentleman, of whom I enquired, " What is
that large establishment we are approaching ?"

" That, sir," he replied, " is Decker's, and I
think it is well worth seeing ; I have often had
a curiosity to enter it myself, and if you like
we can now apply for admission." We drew
up at the gates accordingly and permission to
enter was readily granted by the custodian.

" You will find the ladies at dinner just now,
gentlemen, " he said, " but they will be happy
to see you."

He accordingly ushered us in, and we passed
down between two rows of the occupants, who
were so busily engaged with their meal that
they scarcely noticed our presence. There
were eighty-seven of them, and what struck us
as very remarkable, they were dining in absolute silence. They were variously dressed,
some in black, some in white, but red appeared

to be the favorite color. It was gratifying to notice that none of them wore bangs or idiot fringes, although they all had switches and high projecting horn combs. We asked the superintendent if the ladies were at all restrained in their liberty. "Oh, no," he replied, "they have certain hours of the day at this season for a promenade upon the lawn, although we require them to be regular at their meals three times daily and to be always within doors at night. In summer we are not so strict; in fact they then live most of the time in the open air."

"Are they charity patients?" we asked, "or do they pay for their board and treatment?" "It is true," he answered, "that they do not come here of their own accord, but I do not believe that they could have such home comforts anywhere else. They like their quarters and are willing to pay for them. They do not pay in cash, but you observe that each one has her reticule in which she brings the proceeds of her day's work. We send it down to New York and sell it there." "But I do not see any gentlemen among them," remarked my acquaintance. The superintendent seemed somewhat confused as he replied that establishments of this kind were more profitable when the boarders were ladies. Soon afterwards we left the building expressing our thanks for the courtesy extended to us and taking a note of the sign over the entrance, " Decker's Milk Dairy."

We passed on over the rich meadow lands of a country so well adapted to milk farms by its natural properties and its nearness by railroad to the city. There were many pretty and even elegant and capacious residences, evidently the homes of families who, combining the *utile cum dulce*, must have other means of support besides the proceeds of these farms. Like Mr. Decker, they make lavish expenditures in economy, the result of which is, as many of these gentlemen farmers are ready to admit, a loss to them for what they charitably intend for a benefit to their neighbors in the instructions given. Singularly, however, the uneducated farmer generally prefers his own old way. Not caring for palatial barns, patent fodder and ensilage, he shelters his cows under rough sheds, feeds them on hay in the winter and turns them out to pasture in summer and makes a living from the proceeds, while his experimenting instructor is carrying his yearly account to the debit of profit and loss.

Passing through the town of North Salem, five miles beyond, the apparently religious character of the people made a deep impression upon me. Inquiring of a farmer who was driving along in a wagon by my side, he said that in a population of twenty-five hundred, there were eight different sects, each of course considering itself in the only straight and narrow path to heaven. "But," added my informant, "such a quarrelsome set of cusses you never did see. I guess the trouble is that religion is cut up into such small junks that nobody gets enough of it to do 'em any good."

The border line is not well defined, but I knew that I was now in Connecticut, and that after riding half a dozen miles further, I should come to the village of Ridgefield, the home of my old friend and schoolmate, Dan Adams, where a hearty welcome awaited me.

Dan is a retired physician—not that celebrated advertiser "whose sands of life have nearly run out." I hope there is much sand yet left in the time-glass of my friend. He is

one of those wise men (of whom there are few)
who know that the grasshopper is likely soon
to become a burden, and so contrive to make
his weight light by husbanding their strength.
How few among men know when to leave off
business, and how few there are of these who
can leave it off and be happy! He is one of
this small number to be envied. Twenty years
ago he relinquished his practice in the city, and
retired to this healthy spot. Here, with his
charming family around him, his comfortable
house, his elegant library, his pair of fine
horses, his robust health, he is as happy as
man can wish to be.

After our dinner we two old fellows sat up
far into the still hours of the night, and over a
bowl of punch, such as we used clandestinely
to quaff, talked of our school-boy days and
playmates. We were at school at Amherst in
the year 1829, and every five years we meet
again on the old playground, for the school is
still maintained. There the present generation of boys look with wonder on the old gray-
beards who fall into ranks—thinner ranks, alas,
at every meeting; and when they see us after
roll-call at our regular game of foot-ball, their
astonishment knows no bounds. And I will

tell you what boy—alas, that he has left us—
could best kick the foot-ball, could best wrestle, run fastest, was the most athletic gymnast,
was the most jovial youngster, though perhaps
the laziest student of us all—Henry Ward
Beecher. " John, I never envied anybody but
you," he said not long ago, "and that only
once. It was when you threw the spit ball at
old Master Colton, and hit him square on the
top of his bald head. I always missed him."

We had a festive night, closing it with a
sound sleep, won by exercise and pleasant
reminiscences. In the morning a hearty breakfast, a warm adieu, and then a gallop back to
Mohegan, stopping again for lunch at the castle built by " Hackaliah Bayley, who imported
the first elephant into these U-nited States—
old Bet ; of course you've heard of old Bet."

Now you too have heard the story, if you
have never heard it before, and you know how
two days may be passed enjoyably in the
country in winter, while you are lying in bed,
or loafing at your club, or in the hands of some
doctor whose interest it is not to recommend
to you the practice of equestrianopathy.

2

CHAPTER II.

Notes of a Road Journey from New York to Boston.—The Turnpikes.—Life in the Farming Regions.—Religion in the "Hill Towns."—The "Commercial Room" at Hartford.—An Aged Amherst Instructor. —A Soldier of Napoleon.—The Old Stage House.

I WAS once visiting in Southern California a ranch owned by an old Mexican gentleman who was unavoidably annexed when the territory was acquired by the United States. The proprietor, whose surroundings indicated prosperity although its modern accompaniments were wanting, nevertheless possessed an elegant carriage, which particularly attracted my attention because it was not in keeping with the other accessories of the estate. "That," said my venerable friend, as he tapped it with his cane, "belongs to my granddaughter. She was educated in San Francisco, and I bought

it to please her, but I never use it myself. At
my age of eighty-five it is not safe to take any
risks, so I stick to my saddle." I will not say
that I am so apprehensive of danger, for I
frequently am transported from place to place
in cabs, railway cars, and steamships, but my
chief pleasure in locomotion is when I find
myself, to use a Western phrase, "on the outside of a horse."

I had accepted an invitation to a Thanksgiving dinner at Boston, and as I am the owner of
a thoroughbred mare who might be idle for
want of exercise in my absence, and as I myself
had no business occupation which might not
brook delay, I thought that an appetite for the
turkey would be increased, and that I might at
the same time refresh my memory by the
sight of ancient landmarks, if I should saddle
the mare and ride to my destination.

I am perhaps a relative of one of the most
valued correspondents of *The Evening Post*
—at any rate, I belong to the family of the
Old Boys. I have read with great interest his
reminiscences of the highways and byways of
New York City, and as his country cousin I
proposed to investigate the highways and
byways that connect the metropolis of busi-

ness and wealth with the metropolis of litera-
ture and art.

As a young boy, sixty-five years ago, I had
travelled from Boston to New York in a stage-
coach, and now as an old boy I desired to
retrace my steps. There are few of us who
would not wish to retrace the steps we have
made in such a length of years, to correct our
wanderings and to live our lives over again,
following in the straight line of duty.

I felt assured that after this long interval of
time I could find my way back without much
difficulty, as most of it would be over the old
turnpike roads. I remembered the story that
Long Tom Coffin tells in the "Pilot" of his
wagon trip from Boston to Plymouth and of
"the man who steered—and an easy berth he
had of it ; for there his course lay atween walls
of stone and fences ; and, as for his reckoning,
why, they had stuck up bits of stone on end,
with his day's work footed up ready to his
hand, every half-league or so. Besides, the
landmarks were so plenty that a man with half
an eye might steer her, and no fear of getting
to leeward."

Fanny was never put to harness but once,
and then she kicked herself out of it. I am

glad that she did, for nobody ever tried the experiment with her again. She is a solid beast eight years old, convex chest and long pasterns, weighs in horse parlance "nine hund'd and a half," with a straight back and high withers built up for the purpose. Her value—well, you can't buy her.

She was at Irvington, and thither I went in an early morning train from New York, and started at eleven o'clock across the country to reach the old Boston post-road to New Haven, passing through the charming county of Westchester, the region of the "neutral ground" of the Revolution, made famous by the alternate occupancy of the American and British armies, the wild raids of the cowboys, the capture of André, and the romance of Cooper which has immortalized reality by clothing it in the garb of that enduring fiction, "The Spy."

We were informed that we were now passing through the property of an eminent financier. Before he became the purchaser of these lands along the New York City and Northern Railroad reports were industriously circulated that fever and ague prevailed to an alarming extent. The lands were consequently some a very low price. But after they had been bought there was an immediate sanitary improvement, and they are now perfectly healthy, and are held at a high price.

Riding through the pretty county town of White Plains over fine macadamized roads, bordered by many attractive residences, we came to Port Chester, where we fed our horses and dined, my companion, who had accompanied me thus far, to my great regret returning to Irvington.

I was now upon the old stage road running closely by the side of the railway, but rising frequently over the hills from which far more extensive views of the Sound could be obtained than from the windows of the cars. There is a succession of large towns, villages, and country-houses that have all sprung into life since the days of the old stage-coach. The traveller of those times would recognize nothing now except the waters beyond the shore, and even these are covered by craft which to his eyes would seem strange as compared with the tiny sloops that then answered all the purposes of traffic between the embryo cities of New York ᵃd Boston. Least of all would he understand and t.ᵉaning of those tall poles crossed at their tops, and the network of wires that carry the unspoken messages we cannot hear, and of which they could not dream any more than they could imagine communication with the isolated stars, which may be a reality sixty-five years hence for the boy of seven years who now travels in the cars.

The telegraph poles and wires were as serviceable to me as were the "walls of stone and fences" to Long Tom Coffin. I could not well miss my road to Norwalk where I passed the first night, and to New Haven, my second resting-place. On the third day, from New Haven to Hartford I had the same guidance, but the road was of a character entirely different.

Were it not for those silent monitors, the gray forefathers of Connecticut might, if they could arise from their graves, walk almost from end to end of this old turnpike of thirty-six miles, connecting the former rival capitals of their State, without perceiving even a shadow of change. Perhaps the houses by the wayside may have grown older, but they look as if they never could have been new. Their paint has not worn off, for painted they never were. They are not enclosed by "stones themselves

to ruin grown," for the stone walls stand at the
borders of the road as they were laid up two
centuries ago. Why is it that immortal man
so soon becomes forgotten and unknown, while
these old stone walls stand as they were piled,
and from century to century bid defiance to
the ravages of time?

I am sure that we all look with a reflection
like this on the memorials of the past, and
often ask of ourselves how it can be that he
whose desire it is to live on and to live forever
in this world of happiness which might increase
as year follows year, should be cut off and
consigned to the dust, while these inanimate
things, seeing nothing, feeling nothing, enjoying nothing, should be gifted with a useless
immortality.

Still, as I looked at the faces of some of
those old farmers and talked with many of them
who neither knew nor cared for anything in
the outside world, I almost imagined that they
were the men who had laid up these very walls,
and that they too were stolidly immortal. Certain I was that if their ancestors could come
back to earth, they would be as much at home
and ᴧong their descendants as among the fences
they had built.

What strange ideas those old fellows had of road building. The engineers of their day, if engineers there were, were impressed with the conviction that a turnpike should be built in an absolutely straight line, no matter what obstacles there might be in the way. It never occurred to them that a fly could crawl around an orange with less effort than he would make in crawling over it, and that the distance would be the same. If the spire of the Strasbourg Cathedral had stood in their way, they would not have budged one inch to the right or to the left. Like ancient mariners before great circle sailing was adopted, they fully believed that from east to west was a direct course, and in trying to establish the mathematical axiom that a straight line forms the shortest connection between two given points, they really succeeded in demonstrating its falsity.

People who travel by rail through the new and prosperous towns that border the line between New Haven and Hartford can form all idea of the contrast presented by the old Bos-
Two distinct phases of civilization are ap first
Much has been said lately in the new self at
of the decay of religious observances uctive
England. This is true of places where some

civilization prevails, for the railroad has dealt
a heavy blow upon the theology of our fathers.
One writer says truly that "these eastern coun-
ties of Connecticut are not physically the best
part of the State, but manufactories and railroads have opened new lines of worldly prosperity and have brought in a population that is
little inclined to support religious services."

On my road I passed through many "hill-
towns," and as part of the journey was pursued
on a Sunday, when at some times I followed
the turnpike and at others the road near the railway, I was struck by the marked difference in
the demeanor of the residents. Early in the
morning the Roman Catholics of a railroad
town were on their way to mass, with a view
of compressing their "Sabbath" into an hour
before breakfast, and then devoting themselves
to amusement for the rest of the day. Getting
back into a hill-town a few hours afterwards,
there was a cessation of all work, and not even
werhild dared to amuse itself. The quietude
and thure seemed to have communicated itself
tain I wiouls of men and to the bodies of animals,
back to oelieve that every horse thereabouts
nong tn almanac in his brain, and that he can
and hace with certainty upon his day of rest.

Men, women, and children were soberly wending their way to meeting, keeping step as it
were to the slow tolling of the bell, and happy
indeed were these hill-town people when there
was not heard the discordant clang from a rival
belfry, but all of them were assembled in "the
old meeting-house" as one flock under one
shepherd.

In the olden times it would have been very
wicked to ride on the Sabbath through this
country on horseback. Indeed, I can well remember when such a practice would not have
been tolerated in the immediate neighorhood of
Boston. Riding and driving were both sinful,
but the former was reprehensible in a higher
degree. Sixty-five years ago no one would
have dared to mount a horse on the Sabbath,
and I recollect witnessing the arrest of a coun-
tryman who having sold his load of wood on
Saturday, was unable to return on account of
the rain until Sunday morning. The excuse
was not admitted and he was locked up until
Monday. This happened six miles from Boston in Dorchester, from whence came the first
colony to these hill-towns and settled itself at
Windsor. Its early history is an instructive
study. It may aid us in getting rid of some

very erroneous ideas we have entertained of
the intolerance of our Puritan forefathers, and
we may thereby discern in what this supposed fault really consisted. We shall find
that a more liberal spirit prevailed among the
churches in the seventeenth and eighteenth
centuries than was afterwards exhibited in the
earlier part of the nineteenth century, and perhaps even at the present day. It is true that
there were some terrible preachers like Ed-
wards, who, later on, endeavored to " persuade men by the terrors of the law "; but although the Assembly's catechism was taught
on general principles as a text-book,—which
might as well have been written in Greek or
Hebrew,—and not infrequently, profoundly
soporific, unintelligible, and consequently harmless hydra-headed discourses on original sin
and election were preached in the absence of
such exciting topics as are now at hand, it is
simple justice to the memory of the clergy of
those days to say that in the main, their sermons were practical, conveying to men views
of daily duty which they could not obtain
through the mists of theology. Such was the
teaching, for the most part, of the old ministers of New England. They were honest,

faithful, good men. They were as truly the clergy of an established church as were the bishops and priests of the church from which they had seceded. The law of the state, founded on the pretence of religious liberty, but combining in itself civil and ecclesiastical power, delegated to them an almost absolute control over the religious and secular conduct of their parishioners. If one of them dared to do anything of which the minister might disapprove he became an outcast from society as well as an " alien from the commonwealth of Israel." Whether men belonged to the church or not, they were by statute assessed for the support of the gospel, and unless they " signed off " to become members of other societies, whether they went to meeting or not, they were obliged to contribute for the support of the gospel as preached in the old meeting-house.

It was a most natural desire on the part of the established clergy to keep their flocks from straying into other fields. For this purpose they pursued a policy of conciliation. However much they might for want of other matter preach of " God's plans and his eternal purpose," all that they required of their hearers was a silent assent to what they could not understand as evidences of their faith in things not seen, and that their works should be in accord with the ten commandments, and especially with the eleventh, which they had taken the liberty to add. "Thou shalt go to meeting twice every Sabbath and pay thy parish taxes."

A conformity to this obligation, in addition to a good moral life with due reticence of opinions, afforded sufficient evidence that a man was a Christian. In short, beyond the essential requisite of a good character, the great point which the old ministers endeavored to bring to bear on their parishioners was that they should hold fast to the monopoly of religious observances, and that they should combine to prevent all outsiders from religious action in opposition to it.

These excellent men would not have forgiven me for riding on horseback on the Sabbath day, but I will atone for the offence by preaching from the saddle this sermon in vindication of them, bringing it to a close by quoting the simple yet comprehensive covenant, which they brought with them from their landing-place on the shores of New England, and which was a sufficient rule of practice for them until a more modern theology introduced the bigotry which has been so falsely laid to their charge.

"DORCHESTER,
"Ye 23d day of ye 6th month (1630).

"We, whose names are subscribed, being called of God to join ourselves together in Church communion, from our hearts acknowledging our own unworthiness of such a privilege or of the least of God's mercies, and likewise acknowledging our disability to keep covenant with God or to perform any spiritual duty which God calleth us unto, unless the Lord do enable us thereunto by his spirit dwelling in us, do, in the name of Christ Jesus, our Lord, and in trust and confidence of his free grace assisting us, freely covenant and bind ourselves solemnly, in the presence of God himself, his holy angels, and all his servants here present, that we will, by his grace assisting us, endeavor constantly to walk together as a right ordered congregation or church, according to all the holy rules of a church body, rightly established, so far as we do already know it to be our duty, or shall further understand it out of God's Holy Word, promising first, and above all, to cleave unto him as our chief and only good, and to our Lord Jesus Christ as our only spiritual husband and Lord, and our only High Priest and Prophet and King. And for the furthering of

us to keep this blessed communion with God,
and with his Son Jesus Christ, and to grow up
more fully herein, we do likewise promise,
by his grace assisting us, to endeavor the establishing among ourselves, of all his holy or-
dinances which God hath appointed for his
churches here on earth, and to observe all and
every of them in such sort as shall be most
agreeable to his will, opposing to the utmost of
our power whatsoever is contrary thereunto,
and bewailing from our hearts our own neglect
thereof in former time, and our polluting ourselves therein with any sinful inventions of
men.

And, lastly, we do hereby covenant and promise to further to our utmost power the best
spiritual good of each other, and of all and
every one that may become members of this
congregation, by mutual instruction, reprehen-
sion, exhortation, consolation, and spiritual
watchfulness over one another for good ; and
to be subject, in and for the Lord, to all the
administrations and censures of the congregation, so far as the same shall be guided according to the rules of God's Holy Word. Of the
integrity of our hearts herein, we call God, the
searcher of all hearts, to witness, beseeching
him so to bless us in this and all other enter-
prises, as we shall sincerely endeavor, by the
assistance of his grace, to observe this holy
covenant and all the branches of it inviolably
forever ; and where we shall fail for to wait on

the Lord Jesus for pardon and for **acceptance** and for healing for his name's sake.

Surely in this simple yet comprehensive covenant there was nothing that savored of intolerance.

It is quite true that this region is "not phy. sically the best part of the State." Indeed, there is not much of Connecticut that is physically good, if by that term is understood adaptation to agriculture, especially agriculture which comes into competition with that of the great West. Tobacco and onion culture in the river bottoms is about all that yields a profit.

It is not easy to understand by what process the farmers of these inland districts manage not only to support life, but to clothe themselves and their families with decency, to pay their taxes, and to maintain their churches. Old men tell sad stories of decadence since the railroads destroyed their industry of supplying the city markets. Farms, they say, are not worth one-half of what was their value fifty years ago. What a commentary is this on the claim of the protectionists, that manufactories encourage the farming in their neighborhood! Certainly the manufacturing interest is centred

3

in New England, and all throughout New England the value of farms is decreasing, so that it is only by hard work and strict economy that the farmer is enabled to pay the expenses that this accursed tariff which he is told is kept up for his benefit, entails upon him.

As the people of Berlin, a little town a few miles south of Hartford, have found that there is no money to be made out of land, they have devoted their attention to the chicken industry.

If Mr. Rutherford B. Hayes had been my companion, he would have found a great deal to interest him here. All the barnyards, fields, and roads were overrun with birds, by no means of a feather, but representatives of every possible variety of the domestic fowl. The magnificent Shanghai stalked by the side of the little Bantam, and the other breeds intermingled. The Plymouth Rock seemed to be the finest specimen among them all. One old farmer, who looked as if he had really landed on Plymouth Rock, told me that on Plymouth Rocks he depended entirely for a living. Although the flocks freely congregate, their owners manage to keep the breeds separate. I rode out of the village at sunset, just as the various families, being driven in by the children, were going to roost, and when their cackling died away upon my ear I was again left to the solitude of the old turnpike and to darkness, until the lights of " Har'ford town " shone out before me.

Fanny and I were detained two whole days in Hartford by a storm of wind and rain. The continued patter on the roof of the stable I doubt not was as pleasing to the mare as the lugubrious prospect from the hotel windows was depressing for me. Still, when I called to mind the graphic description given by Irving of his rainy Sunday at a country inn, a true philosophy led me to make a comparison in my own favor.

At any rate, I could look out upon a city street instead of a stable yard, and in place of the melancholy cock standing with drooping feathers on the dunghill, there were people to be seen battling the storm, often with reversed umbrellas, and sometimes swept by the furious gusts around the corner and dumped into the gutters. That, too, was a greater misery than my own, and I confess that the old proverb afforded me no little satisfaction. Besides, within doors I had company. Several drum-

mers or "travellers," as they call themselves,
were also storm-bound. As we were all regis-
tering our names together, the clerk replied to
the question of one as to the charges. "Three
dollars and fifty cents per day is the rate, but
it is two dollars and fifty cents for travellers.
You are a traveller, aren't you?" "Yes, sir,"
he replied. When the same question was proposed to me, my conscience did not forbid
me to answer in the affirmative. So I was
adopted into the fraternity and thereby learned
many of the tricks of the trade. I played
euchre with my fellow "travellers" to while
away the tedious hours. My partner travelled
for a crockery house, and of our opponents one
travelled for a California wine house, and the
other for a patent medicine firm. Others in
the room travelled for dry-goods, grocery,
saddlery, hardware, and all sorts of houses,
one of them for a peanut firm, carrying with
him a large bag of samples, the commodities of
the others being packed in enormous trunks.
My modest roll of baggage astonished them,
and when they asked what my business was, I
told them it was the horse business, and that I
could not very well bring my sample into the
house.

My association with these peripatetic agents taught me that a greater revolution in trade than I had supposed possible had taken place since the days of old. Readers of my own age, and even those many years younger, will remember the Exchanges in our cities where merchants congregated for the transaction of their own business, and how they have long ago been abandoned, a swarm of brokers kindly acting as intermediaries, while the principals sit at ease in their offices and pay them their commissions, which they, of course, charge back again on those poor devils the consumers, who are persons of no account when there is a question of tariff or exactions of any kind whereby a few men may be benefitted at the expense of many.

But it must be admitted that by this comparatively new system of drumming, the country merchant often finds that he can purchase his goods at a cheaper rate than when he was obliged to make his semi-annual tours to the great cities to obtain his supplies. It used to be a costly trip for him, especially when, as was not unfrequently the case, he fell into the hands of the Philistines. One business often ruins another; that of the decoy ducks is

gone ; the city hotels and places of amusement
have suffered, but, upon the whole, the con-
sumer in this case has not suffered, and the
country merchant, although by staying at home
he loses the opportunity of getting brightened
by contact with the outside world, escapes
fleecing and demoralization.

As this is necessarily a personal narrative, I
may be excused for bringing into it a personal
reminiscence to which I was led by the rainy
days at Hartford.

Francis Fellows, a venerable gentleman in his
eighty-third year, resided there, and was still
actively engaged in the practice of law. In
1829 and 1830 he was one of the principals of
a school with a title sonorous, but not more so
than it deserved, of " The Mount Pleasant
Classical Institution," at Amherst. Three
other teachers of a still more advanced age
still live, and all, like Mr. Fellows, are in
good physical and mental condition. This is a
proof that the large number of boys under
their charge treated them kindly, and to-day
those of us who survive hold them in the
highest respect and affection.

I could not lose the opportunity of calling
on my good old friend, and, although I cannot

compare myself in any other respect to the great apostle, I felt that, like him, I was "sitting at the feet of Gamaliel." He seemed to remember the names of all his old pupils and our various characteristics. It was gratifying, because I knew he was sincere, to hear him say that, although he was sometimes obliged to punish us, not one of us ever gave him real pain by our demeanor toward him. "You were a pretty good boy, John, though not one of the best," he said; "you liked play better than study." "You are right, sir," I replied, "and it is as true now as it was then." Enumerating several more, he came to Beecher.

"Beecher," he said, "did not study more than you did, but he was a boy that didn't need to study. He had it all in him ready to break out. The only thing to which he gave any attention was elocution. He learned his gestures at Mount Pleasant, and since that time he has acquired matter to fit them. Yes, he was at the head of his class in elocution, and I believe he was at the head of his class in wrestling and foot-ball. I don't remember that he was remarkable for anything else."

And so the old teacher and the old pupil sat

together and called to mind the memories of
the past and of the school of which I can truly
say, in the words of Lowell at Harvard:
" Dear old mother, you were constantly forced
to remind us that you could not afford to give
us this and that which some other boys had,
but your discipline and diet were wholesome,
and you sent us forth into the world with the
sound constitutions and healthy appetites that
are bred of simple fare."

On the next morning the southerly gale had
blown itself out and a cold north-west wind
was sending the scud flying through the sky.
Fanny, after her rest of two days, trotted
briskly out of the stable yard down through
the streets of " Har'ford town," over the Connecticut River bridge, and on to the frozen
ruts of the country road toward Vernon, the
first town of importance on another turnpike,
the old " Boston and Hartford," a straight,
undeviating line that stretched originally for a
hundred miles from the eastern bank of the
Connecticut to the seaboard, and can even yet
be traced until it is lost among the suburbs of
the metropolis. Before noon we had ascended
its highest point of elevation, 1500 feet above
the sea level, commanding a view of East and

West rocks near New Haven in the south-west, of Holyoke range on the north, of the winding river and of Nipsig Lake, which lay almost directly beneath. For a long distance habitations were scattered and far between.

Somewhat further on I came to a house lonely, unpainted, and yet somehow, I could not tell in what respect, different from any farm-houses I had yet seen, except that there were certain indications of refinement about it, evident, but not easily described. At the little wicker gate before it stood an old man, of whom I inquired as to the distance of the nearest town. He bowed politely and replied with an accent which told me that he was French. He was overjoyed when I addressed him in his native tongue.

"Ah, monsieur," he said, "this is the first time out of my own family that I have heard my own language for the forty-five years that I have lived in this lonely place. Paris, did you say? It is different from this, is it not?"

"Yes, indeed," I replied; "I was there only a few months ago, and I wish you could be there to see the changes in the half-century of your expatriation." And then I poured into his greedy ears the story of the gay boulevards, the charming Champs Elysées, the Bois de Boulcgne, the little steamboats on the Seine, the theatres, and all that makes the bright capital of the world so attractive. The tears coursed down his cheeks as he sighed and said: "So you have seen all that, but tell me, did you see his tomb? I would like to see the tomb of Napoleon more than everything else, and then I would come back to this wilderness to die."

"It is possible," I said, "that when a child you may have seen the Emperor."

"As a child!" he exclaimed. "Look at me; how old do you think I am?"

"Perhaps a little older than myself," I replied.

"Monsieur, my age is ninety-five years," he answered, and then he drew his bent form to its full height, straight like the telegraph pole at his side; his eyes flashed with the brightness of youth, and striking his hand upon his heart, he exclaimed in words whose emphasis will not bear translation: *"Je suis vieux soldat de Napoléon!"*

When I parted from the veteran, he gave me a military salute, and on turning in my saddle to look at him once more, I saw him

standing on the same spot with his arms folded
à *l'Empéreur*, lost in reveries of the past.

Since I have made these notes there has
appeared in the Boston *Herald* an interesting
sketch of the career of François Radoux, born
in Brittany in 1790. He too was a soldier of
the empire, and was living in Portland, Me.
Very likely others still survive in France, but it
is scarcely possible that there are any more of
them to be found in the United States. I
wished that these two "venerable men who
have come down to us from a former generation" might be brought together to embrace
each other and to fight over those old battles
side by side. Their stories would be worthy
of a place in the well-worn war columns of the
Century magazine.

But time marches rapidly on the downhill
grade. I have now to make another note.
Radoux died a few months ago and the *vieux
soldat* whom I met upon the road stands guard
alone on the threshold of the tomb.

I drew up for the night at the hotel in
North Ashford. It was the old stage house of
former days. Evidently no change had come
over it but the change of decay. It stood
close upon the road, with a capacious stable

near by, a porch with side seats at the front
door, a piazza leading around to the bar-room
more frequently entered, planks here and there
missing, the cornices rotted off, blinds for
some windows, half-blinds for others, no blinds
at all for the rest, and before it a gallows sign
with its paint obliterated, so that the form of
Gen. Washington or of a horse, whichever it
may be, could not be traced, swinging and
creaking on its time-worn hinges. The stable,
of course, had my first consideration. Riding
over the grass-grown track to the door, and
kicking against it to call out some sign of life,
a squeaking voice responded, and presently
emerged an old man whose clothes and hair
were covered with hayseed, for he had been
startled from his sleep. Rubbing his eyes
with a dazed expression, like that of *Rip Van
Winkle* as he wakes upon the stage, he inquired: " Who be you, and what do you
want ? "

" I want my horse put up for the night," I
replied.

" Where's your cattle ? "

" Cattle ? "

" Yes, cattle ; ain't you driving ? "

" Driving cattle ? No, I came from New

York, am going to Boston, and intend to stop here to-night."

"You don't tell! Hain't seen the like for more'n forty year. We don't take in a'most nobody but drovers now. Well, ride in. I'll bed your hoss down and feed him. Want hay and oats both, I suppose."

The big door was swung wide open, and I rode into an equine banquet-hall, deserted.

" Plenty of room here," I remarked, as I looked upon the double row of horse stalls, many of which were filled with hay, old harnesses, disjointed wagons, farming tools, and odds and ends of everything.

" Plenty of room; well, yes, I guess there is now, but there wasn't plenty too much room fifty year ago, mister. Every one of them twenty-four hoss stalls had change hosses goin' into and comin' out of em. Oh Lord, oh Lord, how times has changed! How when the mail stage,—Joe Benham he always drove it—and may be two and sometimes three extries, rattled up to the door and the passingers tumbled out to the bar-room and got such new rum as you can't get noways now, and then marched into the eatin' room for their dinners, we hoslers used to onharness the teams, lead

'em smokin' into the stable, harness up the
fresh 'uns, and have 'em all ready for a new
start. Joe, he allers 'sisted on my holdin' on
to the nigh leader till he got up and took the
lines. I can see him now and hear him holler,
'Let 'em go, boy!' And away they went,
down the hill, extries after 'em—Joe, he allers
took the lead cause he car'd the mail—all in a
cloud of dust. Ah, them was the times—
times as was times. Damn the railroads! I
say. Well, you better go into the house, and
Miss Dexter'll git you some supper. Supper's
a'most ready, and I'll be in as soon as I've
bedded down your hoss."

A cheery light was gleaming from the
kitchen and bar-room windows as I entered the
door of the latter apartment, on which the
black-painted letters indicating its specialty,
were still distinctly legible. I was cordially
welcomed, although the same surprise was
manifested that I was not in charge of a drove
of cattle on my way to Brighton. "Has boy
Andrew taken care of your horse?" asked the
landlord.

"I turned her over to an old man in the
barn," I answered.

"Oh, well," he said, "that's all right; that

was boy Andrew. He was a boy in the old stage time when my father kept the house, and he has been boy ever since, and always will be. Supper will be ready soon. I'm right glad to see you. You're welcome to the best we've got if you'll set down with the family. We don't use the big room any more." And then to show it, he opened a door on which " Dining-room " in faded characters often scrubbed over, was still plain enough. That banquet hall too, was long since deserted and used now but occasionally for a country ball to which sleighing parties sometimes come from the neighboring villages and farm-houses. The long table and the chairs had disappeared and all the indications of former occupancy were the worn floors, with here and there the pine knots which refused to wear down.

As I paced up and down the cheerless apartment, a sadness again came upon me such as all men must feel in the reflection that sentient beings like ourselves with throbbing pulses, animal spirits, and thinking brains, once living on God's beautiful earth were now mouldering beneath its ground, and that we who occupy their places must soon follow them, to be followed turn after turn, in the ceaseless round of

existence and death. God only knows why
He made us to live and to die.

Then the great bell which had summoned
those now departed guests to their meals,
called our little company to supper in a small
room adjoining the kitchen. " All we have,"
said the landlady in excuse, " is tea, bread and
butter, milk, tripe, and sausages ; we are ten
miles from the railroad and from any town, and
the butcher comes only once a week, when he
brings the newspaper."

She needed not to make any apology. In
company with the family, including boy Andrew, who entertained me with more reminiscences, I made a hearty meal. Soon afterward
the usual tavern loungers made their appearance. The landlord was in a jovial and generous mood.

" Gentlemen," said he, " we've got a visitor
to-night, and I am going to treat. Liquor
shan't cost any of you a cent. Call for gin or
cider as much as you want. The whiskey is
all out."

The invitation was accepted with alacrity.
" Fetch on your gin," was the general demand.
Afterward we had cider, then gin again, and so
the gin and cider alternated, and if they were

not actually mixed in the glasses, it amounted to very much the same thing. I could fill these pages with the stories that were told in the intervals of the game of " high low Jack," which we played with a pack of well-worn cards, that had done duty, perhaps, ever since the old stage times. But owing to the circumstances, the recollection of these stories is somewhat confusing. It was not exactly one of the *noctes ambrosianæ* of Christopher North, but the enjoyment on an inferior plane was like unto theirs.

The clock, which had been set by my watch—for, unknown to all our friends, to whom it did not matter, it had been nearly an hour out of the way—at length admonished us that the festivities should come to an end. The neighbors bade me a cordial good-by and filed out into the cold air on their homeward tramp, and the landlord, with a tallow dip in hand, conducted me to my room. Again we walked through the dreary dining-hall, and then through a long entry-way, whence opposite the front door a wide staircase with carved balustrades ascended.

Arriving at the top, he opened the door of a large corner room of four small-paned windows

with pendent blue-paper curtains partly rolled
and held by white strings. He said "good-
night," and then I looked around at the threadbare carpet, the bureau with here and there a
knob, the wooden chairs, and the pine table
surmounted by basin and pitcher. But what
especially attracted my attention was the enormous four-post bedstead with fluted columns
rising nearly to the ceiling, the patchwork quilt,
and the valance which hung half way to the
floor. I did not need to open a window for
air. Every sash was loose. The room was
sufficiently ventilated, and it was cold but not
damp, although a fire had not probably been
lighted there for years and years. So I climbed
up to the elevated sleeping plane, and falling
into a deep valley with mountains of feathers on
either side, was soon asleep, notwithstanding
that north-west gale which beat its night-long
tattoo on the rattling window sashes.

After an early breakfast I bade adieu to my
liberal host. Alas for him, he lives ten miles
from a railroad, and knows little of the ways
of the world and of its impositions on the
guileless traveller. I had had two "square
meals," an unlimited supply of gin and cider,
and a bed ; Fanny had had good care, a peck

of oats, and all the hay she could eat, and our bill was one dollar. When I put a quarter into the hands of the boy Andrew, he looked at it intently before he closed his fingers upon it, and remarked : " Wall, you must have plenty o' money. In the old stage times passengers never gin me more'n ninepence, not many of 'em more'n fopence happ'ny, and most of 'em nothin'."

I still followed the turnpike to Hopkinton, where we passed the last night before reaching our destination, and arrived in Boston on the next day, losing all traces of the ancient turnpike on reaching Ashland, about fifteen miles from the city.

We were six days upon the road exclusive of the involuntary detention of two days at Hartford. By our route, which was not so direct as it might have been had I struck across from New Haven, we covered the distance of 211 miles, an average of about thirty-five miles per day, the longest having been thirty-nine miles, and the shortest, which was the last, twenty-eight.

Appetite was not wanting for my Thanksgiving dinner.

CHAPTER III.

The Old Church and the Old Home.—The Pretty Neponset.—Changes in a Boston Suburb.—A Story of Webster.—Notes by the Way.—The Pilgrims and Massasoit.

IT is not so easy to get out of Boston as it was before Boston stretched itself over the surrounding country, leaving the little peninsula on which it was founded, to serve mainly for business purposes, while residences have been built up on the newly acquired territory. Not content with the absorption of Roxbury and Dorchester, the city has brought the more distant country into town by cutting down its hills and transporting them into the Back Bay, which has now become the home of fashion and of æsthetic religion.

Riding out over Washington Street, I call to mind the time when it was "the Neck," I remember when Lafayette entered the city upon it in 1824, and how the high water that day washed upon both sides of the street. Since then Boston has outgrown herself, and has overflowed, because of the foreign tide that has poured in upon her. One can scarcely take up a Boston newspaper without reading columns of reminiscences, in which there is always a touch of sadness, a mourning for departed days. Wealth and splendor, population and even culture, afford no consolation to these desponding antiquarians. The Boston of their fathers, the American Boston, has gone, and a new Boston, a Boston of foreigners, has taken its place. When Dorchester twenty years ago was annexed, it seemed very hard for the people of that ancient borough to give up its name. They thought that Boston should have been annexed to Dorchester, but they were obliged to succumb to numbers, and the alien tide has swept over them too, and has nearly washed out their Puritan Sabbath, to which they held on longer with traditional reverence than almost any other town in Massachusetts.

I ride slowly and reverently by the old meeting-house and by the old homestead where I was born. The latter is sacred to my

own heart, but the former has a history for the
public. Within its walls was blown the first
bugle note of actual war between orthodoxy
and Unitarianism, in 1811. There was open
mutiny, and an attempt to eject by force from
his pulpit the minister who represented the
Trinitarian creed. Then came a division, but
the bitter animosity engendered by this religious strife lasted throughout our childhood
and youth, enforcing a strict taboo upon the
social intercourse of families, throwing a wet
blanket over our juvenile spirits, and encour-
aging no little spiritual pride among us ortho-
dox children, who pitied the Unitarian boys
and girls because they were sure to be damned,
while we could not but envy them for their
better opportunities of enjoying the present
life.

What a commentary it all was upon faith
and works ! Wilcox kept the tavern opposite,
where on Sundays, before and after meeting,
he dispensed rum to his fellow church members. He was a good man because he believed
in the doctrines of the Assembly's Catechism.
If he had denied them, and, conscientiously
closing his bar-room on Sundays, had still led
his otherwise exemplary life, he would have

been condemned to eternal punishment. But he died at peace with his Maker and himself. My father, his pastor, wrote the lines which may be seen upon his gravestone:

With faith and works his life did well accord,
He served the public while he served the Lord.

Not many years after the declaration of doctrinal war, there arose in that old meeting-house another controversy of startling proportions, which impressed itself upon my early childhood. This was the hard-fought stove engagement. The self-denial exercised sixty or seventy years ago for no other purpose than that of escaping future punishment, in going to meeting through a winter's storm, to sit upon hard seats, and to kick our feet upon an uncarpeted floor, the mercury sometimes below zero, through the delivery of much longer sermons than are inflicted upon us now, cannot be appreciated by those who consider it a pleasure rather than a duty to attend churches where they may recline on soft upholstery in a balmy furnace heat, listening to discourses of moderate length and of greater scope and liberality.

Then, families were seen wending their way

to their seats, some of the children carrying in
their hands little tin foot-stoves set in slatted
frames, so that mamma or grandmamma at
least might have some comfort for her toes,
while steaming breaths ascended from the
pews, and the pulpit seemed to be occupied by
a high-pressure engine.

Such was the condition of things in the year
1820 or thereabouts, when some audacious in-
novators proposed the introduction of stoves
with long ranges of pipe for heating the house.
The war was fiercely waged, but fortunately it
did not result in another secession. At last
the stove party was victorious. Old " Uncle
Ned Foster " was foremost in the opposition.
He threatened to " sign off," but finally he
concluded to remain loyal and sit it out. So
on the first Sunday after the stoves had been
introduced, the old gentleman occupied his
pew as usual, the stove-pipe being directly over
him. There he sat with no very saint-like expression throughout the sermon, a red ban-
danna handkerchief spread over his head, and
his face corresponding to it in color. A general smile circulated through the house, the
minister himself catching the infection, for
almost everybody excepting Uncle Ned was

aware that, the day being rather warm, no fires had been lighted.

I have gone back many, many years. There has not been so much change during all this time in the old elms, the stone walls, and even in the houses, but generations have gone and come and gone again in these threescore years and ten. We remember the places, but " the places that once knew them shall know them no more."

Just beyond the old church is a house which has undergone various transformations and is now a hotel. It was once occupied by Daniel Webster. It brings to mind the first ride on horseback that I can remember. Like all stolen fruit it was sweet, and like stolen fruit it left a bitter taste. Fletcher Webster and I, little fellows of about seven years old, used to go to school to Master Pierce on Milton Hill. As our house was on his way, Fletcher was accustomed to call for me in the morning, and we returned together in the afternoon, being boarded out for dinner in the neighborhood of the school-house at the rate of twelve and one-half cents each for our meals. Saturday afternoon of course " school did not keep."

One Saturday morning Fletcher came riding

up to our door bareback on his father's beautiful black mare. " Jump up behind, Johnny,"
he cried ; " father's gone to Boston, school will
be out, and we'll get back before he gets
home!" So Fletcher and I rode off down
through the village, across the bridge, and up
the hill for the rest of a mile to the school. I
am not sure whether the mare ran away with
us or not. We did not care, and we were very
happy. We tied Bessie to a tree in a clump
behind the school-house and went in to apply
ourselves diligently to our lessons. An hour
afterward, Master Pierce had a class up for
recitation. It was a warm day. The windows
and doors were open. Suddenly Mr. Webster
stalked into the little school-room. I am
pretty sure that I shall not live to the age of
Methuselah, but if I do I shall not forget that
scene. The class stopped their recitation.
Master Pierce stood still and the ruler dropped
from his hand making the only noise that
broke the dead stillness. Mr. Webster walked
up to his son and said in a deep tone, not so
very loud, but which seemed to me like a clap
of thunder, " Where's the mare!" and then he
lifted Fletcher from his seat by the ear. He
told me afterward that his father said nothing

more at the time or when he came home. He merely went with him to the tree where the mare was tied, unhitched her, tied her behind his chaise, and drove off.

Leisurely and sadly two little boys walked home from school, and ever afterwards, going and coming, they walked.

Fanny and I again went over the road that the two school-boys had so often travelled sixty-six years ago, down through the village, across the bridge, and up the hill. In all this time there has scarcely been a change. Boston has spread itself everywhere but here. There by the roadside is the cemetery, the " burying-ground, " as it is still called. There lie the early settlers, and should they rise from their graves to-day, they would recognize the surroundings. There are few new houses in Milton Lower Mills village ; the amber-colored water pours over the dam with the same ceaseless music to meet the salt tide of the Neponset that flows to its base ; the same odor of fresh water brought from its course above, and of the chocolate ground at the mills, pervades the air, for memory treasures the fond associations of all our senses. What country child grown to old age does not remember the sweet

briar, the syringa, or the tansy by the wayside
of his home?

Everything of sixty-six years ago was still
where it was till we came to the site of the
little school-house, but the school-house is not.
More than half a century has passed since
Master Pierce was gathered to his fathers.
Daniel Webster's name alone is immortal.
His son, my little schoolmate, died upon the
battle-field, a sacrifice to the country that was
so ungrateful to his illustrious sire, while those
of us who survive them may thank God for
the memories of the life that has passed, for
the good in the life that now is, and for the
hope of the life to come.

It is all like the little river we have just
crossed, which has meandered for miles
through rich meadows, bringing away the col-
ors of their grasses and their flowers brightened by the sunlight falling upon the quiet
basin in which for a time it rests until it leaps
over the falls and loses itself, as all rivers are
lost at last, in the embraces of the boundless
sea.   But is the pretty stream lost merely because it has poured itself into the ocean?
Does it not yet live in my memory and in
thousands of other memories besides?   It is

one of those things of beauty that are joys forever. Exhaled to the skies, it may float "a
sun-bright glory there," and wafted to another continent, may dance down from the
summits of the Alps and water the valleys of
Switzerland. No, there is nothing lost.
When we ourselves, less useful in the world
than its rivers, shall drift away into the ocean
of eternity, we, like them, may be exhaled to
serve a better purpose in some other sphere
of the universe.

Half mounting Milton Hill, we turn to the
right, entering upon the old Taunton turnpike, and keeping a southerly course for a few
miles, gain the highest point, which is in the
notch of the Blue Hills. Approaching it, and
afterwards descending the southern slope as
the mist hangs over the neighboring hills, it
required little effort of the imagination to
transport one's self to the White Mountains
or the Sierras, so charmingly delusive was the
scenery as it was thrown out of proportion by
the hazy atmosphere. Thus we may travel
away many miles at a very cheap rate, and
when the sun breaks out, we may come as
easily home.

For long reaches this old turnpike is little

travelled. In some places the trees have
sought companionship in their loneliness, leaning over to each other and intertwining their
branches. Then again are long, barren
stretches, small villages with meeting-houses
that were painted once, blacksmiths' shops
where anvils ring no longer, "English and
West India Goods Stores" which have not
many English or West India goods to sell, because population is wanting, for farms are now
valueless. Occasionally as we mount a hill we
get a view of towns a few miles upon the left,
the Randolphs and the Bridgewaters, with
their shiny-spired churches and clustered
white houses and shops, manufacturing towns,
prosperous at the expense of other people, and
in the distance we hear the triumphant shout
of the iron horse and the clatter of his hoofs.

Taunton, or Tar'n, as it is called by the natives, is one of these thriving factory towns :
and, moreover, it is an exceedingly pretty town,
but its chief attractions for us were a good
stable and a well-kept hotel, where it was
convenient to pass the night, as we had accomplished somewhat more than half the distance
that separates Fall River from Boston.

We jogged along leisurely on the next day,

for we had not much more than twenty miles to go over, and the snow which had fallen in the night, and was still falling, rendered Fanny very uncomfortable on her feet.

There is little of interest upon the road, bleak as it is in winter and scarcely less so in summer. What brought our fathers to these inhospitable shores is a question often asked, and generally answered by attributing their coming to a special dispensation of Providence. If there ever was such a thing as a special Providence, it manifested itself in the settlement of the colonies of Plymouth and Narragansett Bay. Although this part of the country was settled later than the neighborhood about Boston, it now has the appearance of a greater age. It was a rough country to live in, and a rough country to die in, as stony fields and grave-stones to this day attest. To look at this ground now, whose great crop is of rock—grass and pasture land being exceptions to the general features of the landscape—we can imagine its utter desolation before any clearings were made. Who of us would have taken such a wilderness in this cruel climate as a gift, and would have risked his life in fighting savages for the maintenance of such a possession ?

The truth is that the Pilgrims came here
by accident, but when once they had settled
down, they determined to make the best of it.

In Young's "History of the Pilgrims," if I
remember aright the authority, we are told
that the company of the *Mayflower* were in the
habit of splitting their wood upon the quarter-
deck, and when the axe was not in use, they
laid it in the binnacle alongside of the compass,
which was so affected by the iron, that the ship
instead of bringing up at the Capes of the
Delaware or the Chesapeake, made the land at
Cape Cod. The passengers could not well get
away, and so, like the fox who had lost his tail,
they made a virtue of necessity, persuading
themselves and others whom they induced to
come after them, that this was indeed a goodly
land.

Robert Cushman, who was a sort of Com-
missioner of Emigration, issued an address to
the English Puritans in 1621, in which he set
forth the attractions of this land flowing with
milk and honey, with all the persuasiveness of
a railroad pamphleteer of the present day. He
was also a prototype of Mr. Henry George in
his theory of agrarianism. He had no more
regard for the rights of the Indians than Mr.

George entertains for those of the proprietors of real estate.

He says: "Their land is spacious and void, and there are few who do but run over the grass as do also the foxes and wild beasts. They are not industrious, neither have art, science, skill, or faculty to use either the land or the commodities of it ; but all spoils, rots, and is marred for want of manuring, gathering, ordering, etc ? As the ancient patriarchs therefore removed from straiter places into more roomy, where the land lay idle and waste, and have used it though there dwelt inhabitants by them (as Gen. xiii., 6, 11, 12 and xxxiv. 21, and xli., 20), so it is lawful now to take a land which none useth, and make use of it."

Thus the Puritans quoted Scripture, and their descendants act upon the same lack of principle without their canting hypocrisy when they drive the Indians from the reservations they have conceded to them. But our ancestors were filibusters in some respects of a more honest type than those of the present day. They merely wanted a little corner of the "spacious and void land" for themselves, and were willing to leave the natives in possession of all the rest. They endeavored to

Christianize them. Eliot translated the Bible into their language. It was a labor of years, and when it was completed, the tribes for whom it was intended had died out, but still the credit for it is due to that devoted missionary.

The Puritans were always ready to make treaties and compromises before they resorted to war and extermination. They behaved much better in this respect than the Israelites, by whose example they justified themselves, and than their own descendants, who make treaties but do not respect them.

As we travel over this wide and stone-walled road along the banks of the river, beholding the smoke of factories and hearing the noise of machinery and railroad-engines, let us close our eyes and ears to the surroundings, and go back in our thought to the time when all this was a wilderness, and to the journey made by Hopkins and Winslow a few months after the colonists landed at Plymouth. It is graphically related by Winslow himself, and the whole story may be found in the interesting work of Dr. Young, to which reference has already been made. Over the ground where I was riding, these two bold men, escorted by a savage, went to visit Massasoit, who dwelt upon yonder hill called Mount Hope.

This is the way the chief entertained them: "Victuals he offered none, for indeed he had not any. He laid us in the bed with himself and his wife, they at one end and we at the other; it being only planks laid a foot from the ground and a thin mat upon them. Two more of his men for want of room pressed by and upon us, so that we were more weary of our lodging than of our journey."

Subsequently, Winslow gives a graceful narration of their journey to Mt. Hope, repeated three years later. Their object in visiting the sachem again, was to comfort and relieve him in his illness. Their kindness was amply rewarded, for whereas Massasoit was perhaps likely to be influenced against the English by other chiefs and by their jealous neighbors the Dutch, the disinterested benevolence added to the medical skill of Winslow and his companions, so touched his heart that no representations against the colonists could afterwards have the least effect upon this noble and grateful soul.

Policy would have dictated the easy extermination of the whites, but gratitude was a

more powerful motive with him than the self-
protection which might properly have been
called patriotism. In whatever light the character and conduct of Massasoit may be viewed,
there is little doubt that his recovery from
illness through the instrumentality of Winslow
contributed largely to the firm establishment
of the Puritans and to the ruin of the Indian
tribes. When Massasoit died, and Philip, a
wiser if not a better man, endeavored to destroy
the colonists in 1675, he found that it was too
late. The cruel Philip was more patriotic than
the gentle Massasoit.

Fanny and I were more concerned with the
present than with all this that happened two
centuries and a half ago. Evening was drawing
on and the snow was beginning to fall thick
and fast. Go on, Fanny, carry me a little
further, and then the good steamer *Bristol* shall
carry us both to New York.

CHAPTER IV.

The Railway Car, the Sleigh, and the Saddle-horse.—Preparations for the Ride.—New York Surroundings.—Reminiscence of Irving.—English and American Country Homes.

"O Winter, ruler of the inverted year;
　Thy scattered hair with sleet like ashes filled,
　Thy breath congealed upon thy lips; thy cheek,
　Fringed with a beard made white with other snows
　Than those of age, thy forehead wrapped in clouds,
　A leafless branch thy sceptre—and thy throne,
　A sliding car, indebted to no wheels,
　But urged by storms along its slippery way,
　I love thee, all unlovely as thou seem'st,
　And dreaded as thou art."

IT was a cold January day when I started from the stable in Fifty-ninth Street for a visit to the country. Railway travelling at this season of the year is especially dangerous. Axles are more liable to break. Three fearful accidents from this cause had lately been recorded. For years after the introduction of

railroads in England, orders were given to
reduce the speed on frosty days, but now,
although the risk is the same, speed is considered to be of more importance than human
life. So we rattle on, satisfying ourselves
from statistics that the average of death from
such causes is small, and calculating with rea-
sonable probability that we shall not be
counted among the dead. The same theory
prevails as to the warming and lighting of
cars. The great mortality from train wrecks
comes from the overturning of stoves and the
bursting of kerosene-oil lamps. But who con-
siders that? We estimate the averages, and
feel reasonably sure that we shall not be
among the victims.

Aside from the danger from a stove, the
stove is a villanous thing anywhere, notably
in a railroad car. It burns up the oxygen of
the air, and is accountable for much of the
pneumonia which at the present day hurries
people out of life. As an abomination it is
second only to steam-pipes.

Englishmen know some things better than
we do. We can teach them something about
baked beans, the frying-pan, a beneficent pro-
tective tariff, and more, but in sanitary science

they are our superiors. You will never find a
stove in an English railway carriage. Their
idea is that it is quite sufficient to keep the
feet warm and not to exhaust the lungs or
stupefy the brain. Passengers are provided
with cylinders of hot water, renewed as occasion requires, on which to place their
feet ; they are therefore safe from stove accidents. In the early railroad days of this country the cars were lighted by enormous candles,
giving all the illumination that was necessary
for ordinary purposes. If the car was over-
turned, the candles extinguished themselves
without causing any damage. But the insati-
able greed for reading, to which the newsboys
so much contribute, has supplanted the inno-
cent candle with the murderous kerosene
lamp, which in a collision scatters destruction
far and wide. The public must be accommo-
dated at the risk of their eyes at all times, of
their lives sometimes ; and when disasters
come, the railroad company is blamed, justly
in a degree, but unjustly inasmuch as the very
thing complained of is demanded by this inex-
orable public.

All this is not irrelevant. If it shall be productive of good to call attention to it, it will

be better than anything else I may have to
say. Besides, I am making my point. In winter it is better to travel by some other means
than the railway.   Sleigh-riding comes next.
That is not immediately dangerous, although
severe colds, conducive to fatal results, may
be contracted. I will admit that there is a certain degree of pleasure in it. At least, it was
pleasurable in former days. One of its attractions for me has been lost since we hear no
more the merry jingling of those great round
bells that were banded over the horse's back.
It is not now the fashion to carry them, and if
anything supplies their place, it is a tinkling
plaything, heard by the foot passenger just as
he is about to be run over.

There are still some of those old Dutch and
New England sleighs existing only as curiosities.   They were made for comfort rather
than for speed.   The fancy sleighs of to-day
have scarcely more back support than summer
trotting wagons.   They are provocative of
rheumatism and kidney complaints. The seat
has hardly room for more than one person,
and if two occupy it, it is greatly to their dis-
comfort. This is not sleigh-riding as we used
to understand it. "Boxes" were they, those

old sleighs? Perhaps so, but very comfortable boxes, high-backed, protecting the shoulders and the neck, high sided, bottoms deeply covered with straw; they were sleighs we got into, not upon; there was abundance of room for a companion, and when we were ensconced in that box and so covered over with buffalo skins that nobody could see exactly what we were doing, and a merry song chimed in with the music of those big bells, that was sleigh-riding—with warm hearts instead of cold backs and freezing toes.

There are two modes of healthful locomotion left to us, pedestrianism and horseback exercise. I make no account of the unnatural bicycle, which doctors tell us is productive of serious disorders when used to excess. Walking is a solitary entertainment. It has no variety in its measured step, although it is valuable for its economy when time is not considered. But there is the companionship of the horse, and the change of gait bringing many muscles into play, which give a peculiar zest to riding. In summer the rapid motion prevents a concentration of the sun's rays, but it is in winter that it starts the blood into circulation, and if the nose becomes red, the cheeks are red also and the glow of health pervades the whole body. With proper precautions, the rider needs not to suffer from cold even in the severest weather.

The mercury stood fifteen degrees above zero when I started from the stable on my ride. I cannot call to remembrance the novel, but it is one of Scott's, where the hero is about to start for the Highlands in company with an old farmer, who, before commencing the journey, carefully wraps the steel stirrups with straw for the purpose of keeping their feet warm. I have always remembered the hint, and have found the practice to be effectual. Avoid at all times, on foot or on horseback, especially on horseback, the unhealthful India-rubber boot or shoe. They are inventions of the undertaker. If you would keep your feet warm and dry, put on thick-soled boots of thick upper leather too, not by any means tight, and wear thin cotton socks with woollen socks over them, and when riding in very cold weather, felt overshoes over the boots. These are not in general use, and I have had some difficulty in obtaining them. In response to numerous inquiries, the shoe-dealers told me that they had not this article. At last a face-tious shop-keeper said that he had plenty of felt slippers, and that he had one pair made for a Chicago girl which were not large enough for her, but he thought they might go on over my boots. They did. So much for stirrups and boots.

To change to the head. Put your soft felt hat in your pocket. Wear a toboggan cap, which may be pulled down over your ears, and over your nose if need be, while you look through the meshes. Wear a cardigan jacket, and button your pea-jacket tightly around your neck. Carry your stable-blanket in this wise, remembering that you are to use a McClellan saddle, as I counselled you to do not long ago; double the blanket, and, leaving just enough to go under the saddle, allow the most of it to fall over the horse's neck till you are mounted. Having mounted, pull the remainder of it over your legs, and start, for now you are ready. You may face snow-storms and blizzards, and you will actually enjoy them as I did.

I was bound to Irvington, for my first stopping place, and after riding through the park, and bestowing pity upon some friends whom I met perched upon their skeleton sleighs, vainly

imagining that they were enjoying themselves,
I struck out upon Jerome Avenue, which
appeared to be leading in the right direction ;
but I soon found that I was heading for
Woodlawn, the city of the dead, for a sarcastic
milkman informed me that I was going all
right if I wanted to be buried, but that if I
wanted to live a little while longer, and to get
to Irvington before night, it would be better to
strike across the country and find Broadway.

I don't think any cockney has an idea of the
crooked lanes that have been laid out, like the
streets of Boston by cows, within a few miles
of New York. I would sooner take my chance
of getting anywhere on a Western prairie than
of finding my way out of town above Harlem
without assistance. However, Fanny and I,
by a combination of instinct, moderate intel-
ligence, and persistent inquiry, at last came in
sight of the North River, and headed up
stream. It was Broadway, as it is called until
it reaches Albany—not the Broadway of salted
railroad tracks and dirty slush, bordered by
shops and hotels; but a Broadway now of
clean white snow, in summer of macadamized
road, shaded by oaks, elms, firs, and pines.
Now, the bare limbs of the great trees form a

network through which we see the Hudson, beautiful at all seasons, and the evergreens, festooned with their wintry robes glittering in the sunlight, are clothed in their gayest attire.

From New York to Poughkeepsie, and even beyond, there is a constant succession of comfortable, elegant, and sometimes ostentatious country houses, owned by New York citizens, many of them, chiefly of the latter class, occupied merely as summer residences. The comfortable and the elegant, which are by no means separate or incompatible, mostly prevail, and the good taste of their owners inclines them to live in them all the year round.

There are many things that are "English, you know," and there is nothing more ridiculous than American servile imitations of foreign customs when they are not adapted to our country or to our circumstances. But there is much that we can learn from England, and the refusal to avail ourselves of English example when it points out an improvement in our society or condition is almost as absurd as toadyism and preposterous imitations of language and dress. The English country gentleman has been an " institution," yes, he has been instituted, fixed, established in Britain for centuries. The English castle and manor-house have been and are still the scenes which English novelists most delight to picture. Comfort, that charming English word for which there is no French equivalent, is centered in them.

Beautiful as they are in summer, with their parks and green lawns, it is in the winter that they are at their best. It is in the winter that people "run down to the country" for their most perfect enjoyment. Christmas was made for the country. Those Christmas holidays! That blessed season of family reunions, of unbounded hospitality, of universal benevolence commemorating the birth of Christ as he would have it observed! He may have been the predicted "man of sorrows and acquainted with grief," but if I read his history aright, he who feasted with Pharisees, publicans, and sinners alike, was of a temperament so happy and genial that he would look with more favor on gatherings like these than upon the life-long fasts and penances of fanatical priests and saints. Christmas, merry Christmas! Yes, he intended that it should be merry. He meant that man should be happy, not miserable, for it was from misery that he came to redeem him.

If English writers have done so much to impress us with the joys of their country life, the purest writer of the purest prose in America has surpassed all of them in such descriptions. Where, then, should he be more appreciated than by those who dwell about his old home! Truly, the proverb is sometimes at fault. This prophet is held in honor in his own country. I once visited him at Sunnyside. It was Sunnyside. He must have unconsciously named it for himself, for he was the sunshine of all around him.

Among all classes along the bank of the Hudson he was personally known and loved. A few days before we called upon him he had been strolling about the country and had inadvertently crossed a farmer's field. The owner, supposing him to be a tramp, had ordered him off with coarse and insolent words; but having discovered his mistake, he came to the cottage to offer his apology in most abject terms. "I was very sorry," said the courteous old man— "not because of what he had said to me in the first instance, but for his needless humiliation when he came to see me. However, I think that in future anybody may walk over his grounds without being molested, for he promised me that, and so I am more than even with him."

The writings of Irving and his dwelling at Sunnyside have built up many Bracebridge Halls in his neighborhood. Into one of them I was thus pleasantly introduced. Riding up the hill leading to Riverdale I was overtaken by another horseman. Acquaintance on the road is often made by complimentary remarks upon the animals we ride. Thus, " That is a nice pony of yours," to which the reply is returned, " Yes, and I was just noticing the pretty head of yours." The ice of conventionality is at once broken and the stream of conversation flows on. Men can commit themselves to it without compromising their characters. It is different with women. They institute and undergo a great deal of preliminary examination. Women have less confidence in each other than men. They go to church more frequently and call themselves miserable sinners with more sincerity. But they are not such miserable sinners as we are. They are vastly better, and yet they are more afraid of contamination from each other. Before they will make any advances, they take long and accurate surveys of physiognomy, contour, and dress, listening with all their ears for an indication of good or bad breeding in the language the object of avoidance or association may use in addressing a third party, and if such an one be not present, perhaps to the orders given to a waiter at the table. The ice to be broken is much thicker than ours, but when it once is broken, the stream flows on with a rapidity that it is impossible for us to match.

" You will hardly get to Irvington in time for lunch," said my young friend. " Here is the avenue leading to our house and I am sure that my mother and family will be glad to welcome you." The invitation was accepted with the cordiality with which it was given and thus a delightful addition was made to the store of my country friends.

It was through the gate-way of an avenue leading to another mansion like unto that where I had been so pleasantly entertained, that as evening was advancing, I turned my horse, arriving under the *porte-cochère* just as my genial host was driving up in his sleigh from the station, and as the. young people were

6

coming in from their healthful exercise of coasting.

It was scarcely the time to draw the curtains over the homelike scene of a blazing wood fire throwing alternate lights and shadows upon the ceiling, and glowing upon the faces of the ladies of the household, to whom notice had been given by the jingling bells that it was the hour for the " five o'clock tea." That, too, is " English, you know," and it is one of the choice importations from the old country, to which not even the most selfish protectionist of home customs who has felt its soothing influence can object. Let temperance people also make a note of it, for it is coming to take the place of the appetizing cocktail. The city resident cannot fully appreciate it. To give it zest it needs the transition from the frosty air to the snug comfort of the country home, from the out-of-door twilight to the interval within doors when there is a suspension between day and night, when there is yet light enough to see, but not light enough to read. That is it exactly ; that is the intervening half-hour when business cares fade away and domestic joys take their place.

"Now stir the fire and close the shutters fast,
Let fall the curtains, wheel the sofa round,
And while the bubbling and loud-hissing urn
Shoots up a steaming column, and the cups
That cheer but not inebriate wait on each,
So let us welcome peaceful evening in."

I am a cosmopolitan. I can dine anywhere
—even at a railway station. I am used to
being summoned to dinner by the sound of
bell or gong, to seeing all the supplies, from
soup to ice-cream, piled upon the table at
once; used to everything, for I was once used
to cutting my share of salt junk from the kid
with my sheath knife ; but now, although I do
not think that any one has the right to re-
proach me with æstheticism, I like to see a
well-dressed butler—not a flunky, but one
who is valuable for his usefulness, and not
disgusting because of his superciliousness—I
like to see such an one open the door and
make his bow, to hear him announce that the
dinner is served. I know that in this Bracebridge Hall there is a meaning in it.

Excessive is the politeness of the garçon of
a French table d'hôte as he appears with
napkin over his arm, but we have no assurance
that the dinner will commend itself to us. I

once heard the question of diet discussed.
There were various theories suggested as to
carbonaceous, and nitrogenous food, the di-
gestibleness of some things, the indigestible-
ness of others.   But it seemed to me that the
question was settled by a bright, intelligent,
healthy woman who observed : " I don't think
it makes so much difference what or how much
we eat.   It all depends on the company with
whom we eat it."   Certainly in this case that
chief requisite was at hand, with all the taste-
ful appointments of the table.

More I will not say of the charming hospitality of my friend and of his family, of the
delightful evening in his library, where I saw
nothing of the books but their covers, for
social intercourse was to me more agreeable
than anything they might contain.   Nor will I
say much of the billiards at which later on I
gained but an occasional victory, nor of the in-
ternal night-cap, the dreamless night, the substantial breakfast, the kind good-byes, the cordial invitation to come again, which I never
decline.   I have sought to give a sketch of
American country houses in the winter.   It is a
family picture which may be reproduced in
the memory of my readers, and I trust that

its general traits are so familiar to them that
I shall not have done violence to the modesty
of my hosts by taking their homes for illus-
trations.

CHAPTER V.

*The Hudson in Winter.—Snow Pictures.—
Castles and Ruins.—The River Towns.—
Story of André.— Legend of Sleepy
Hollow.—The Grave of Irving.*

IT was a bright frosty morning when Fanny
and I left Irvington—upward bound along
the eastern bank of the Hudson.   More snow
had fallen during the night covering the
sleigh tracks on the road, and now the fresh
north-west gale set the storm again in motion
from the ground, whirling the snow in fantastic wreaths and shaking it down in huge
flakes from the overladen firs.   It was somewhat blinding to the eyes and cutting to the
cheeks, it is true, but one is always willing to
pay a fee for a view of a fine picture, and this
trifling inconvenience was but a small tribute
to Nature for the exhibition of her wonderful
panorama of field and woodland, hills and distant mountains, with the broad intervening
86

river, whose surface, like everything far and near, was covered with a mantle that sparkled in the sunlight.

It has been often said with truth that all that is needed by our river to make it as picturesque as the Rhine or the Rhone, is history and its accompaniments. We have now the green banks, the widened lakes, the narrow channels, palisades, and highlands, as beautiful and as romantic as theirs ; but they tell us that we have no such castles and ruins. Still we are making the attempt to equal them. Greystone, for instance, represents a castle with some effect. It has not the merit of ugliness certainly, but from its commanding height it is quite as desirable a structure to the eye as if it had more of fancied architectural merit and had been built a thousand years ago. We are trying our 'prentice hand at ruins, too. Our great landscape painter, Bierstadt, has offered an unwilling contribution to such scenic effect. A few miles above Greystone, perched upon a high hill on the opposite side of the road, stood his stately mansion. The fire has been more powerful than his brush. It has made a picture that can be seen for miles around, of lone chimneys and blackened walls, such as the

American tourist would hail with rapture if he should get a glimpse of them from a steamboat on the Rhine.

Time will perhaps bring us our share of ruins, and then the Hudson will meet the approbation of the antiquary and the tourist ; but the lover of nature cannot reverse the engine of progress and turn the wheels of the ages back to the past. He can never see the Hudson again as he may see the Columbia now, rolling down through its forests, its silence broken only by the thunder, the storm, and the screams of wild fowl and beasts.

Nor is it certain that the future has anything in store to replace this charming picture of the past. There are not likely to be any enduring ruins. Every stone of a dismantled building will be utilized by our practical descendants for a new house, for a railroad, or a garden wall, and the Hudson will never be more beautiful and attractive than it is to-day.

These river towns are all much alike, sloping down from the Broadway road to the water-side with the same gradations, country-seats of the rich from the city, comfortable homes of the " well-to-do " residents, stores and shops, rookeries, saloons, and coal-yards, which border on the railroad and the river. Thus, society is defined by the grade of the land, and the two extremes would be antagonistic did not the happy medium preserve the balance.

In the olden time most of the population was located by the docks for commercial convenience, the dwellers upon the stage-road above subsisting on what they gained as hangers-on around the tavern and the stables. Most of those old caravansaries have long ago been demolished or put to other uses. The Vincent House, however, still holds its own on the turnpike at Tarrytown, modernized somewhat, but yet affording entertainment for man and beast.

When I stop, as I sometimes do, and enter its bar-room with motive undisguised, I meet the faces of men whom I have known for years, fixtures there—men who know everything, because their fathers and grandfathers knew everything, and told it to them, about Revolutionary times. They do not agree in their knowledge, but that is a matter of small account. "Them fellers that captured André," said one of them, "were part of a gang of Skinners. You needn't talk; shut up. I've heard my gran'ther tell all about it, and don't

you s'pose he knew? André he didn't have
money enough about him. That was what
was the matter ; and they cal'lated, they did,
that Gen. Washington's cash was better than
the Britisher's promises."

" Well, hain't I heard my gran'ther talk about
it, too?" responded another resident of the
bar-room. " He knowed 'em, he did, individ-
ooally, and he said that if André's stirrups,
saddle, horse, and all had been made of solid
gold, and he'd offered it to 'em, they wouldn't
have looked at it no more than they would at a
copper cent."

" I've hearn' tell," chimed in a little old man,
" that the trouble with André was that he was
out o' rum, and they wanted him to treat, and
he couldn't. 'Tell you, if he had a got off it
would a been a lesson for him in future—never
git out o' rum. Ef his flask had not gin out,
he could have said : ' Come, boys, let's set down
here on the bank, take a drink, and talk over
things good-natured.' There would not have
been no occasion for pulling off his boots."

This suggestion was new to me, but the pro-
pounder was not, perhaps, far out of the way
in his general idea that a little more tact
would have saved André. Dr. Coutant, an

intelligent physician of the town, who has gathered a fund of information pertaining to the early history of Westchester County, does not credit the captors with any patriotic motive.

There is documentary evidence, made public by the Rev. Daniel W. Teller ten years ago, which settles the question absolutely, and displays the conduct of the three "patriots," in a worse light than it had ever been viewed before. The gravest accusation that previously had been made against them was that before they knew anything more of their prisoner than that he was a British officer, they had expressed their willingness to release him if he could offer them a sufficient inducement in money; but it now appears that after having discovered the compromising papers in his boot, they agreed upon a sum of 500 or 1000 guineas as his ransom, and that the negotiation failed simply because they could not obtain satisfactory security that it would be paid. Gen. Washington was not aware of all that had transpired between André and his captors when he made his first report, in which he says:—

"A combination of extraordinary circum-

stances and unaccountable deprivation of mind
in a man of the first abilities, and the virtue of
three militia men, threw the Adjutant General
of the British forces (with full proof of
Arnold's intention) into our hands; and but
for the egregious folly or the bewildered con-
ception of Lieut.-Col. Jamison who seemed
lost in astonishment and not to have known
what he was doing, I should have gotten
Arnold."

The militia men took André to Jamison,
and Jamison, who seems never to have been
suspected of complicity in the treason,
although that is the only rational way of ac-
counting for his conduct, despatched André
with a guard to Arnold himself, sending him
a letter detailing the circumstances of the
capture, but transmitting the compromising
papers to Washington who was upon his route
from New England.

Maj. Talmadge soon afterwards arrived at
Jamison's quarters and having convinced his
superior officer of his stupidity, started in pur-
suit and brought André back, but strangely
permitted the messenger to proceed with
the letter. The result was that Arnold
effected his escape, and on the second day

after André's arrest he was brought to the quarters of a young lieutenant of the Second Regiment of Light Dragoons, under Col. Sheldon. Lieut. King, at that time scarcely of age, appears to have conducted himself with remarkable discretion and to have shown his good breeding as a gentleman. He afterwards became a general, and served with honor through the war.

"In the year 1817," says Mr. Teller, writing in 1877, "Gen. King was written to by a friend who desired to know the exact facts in relation to Maj. André's capture, etc. The following letter was written by Gen. King in reply, and, although previously solicited for publication, is now for the first time given to the public":

RIDGEFIELD, June 17, 1817.

DEAR SIR:
Yours of the 9th is before me. The facts, so far as I am acquainted with them, I will state to the best of my ability or recollection. Paulding, Williams, and Van Wort I never saw before or since that event. I know nothing about them. The time and the place where they stopped Maj. André seems to justify the character you have drawn of them. The truth is, to the imprudence of the man and not the patriotism of any one is

to be ascribed the capture of Maj. André. I was the first and only officer who had charge of him while at the headquarters of the Second Regiment of Light Dragoons, which was then at Esq. Gilbert's in South Salem. He was brought up by an adjutant and four men belonging to the Connecticut militia, under the command of Lieut.-Col. Jamison, from the lines near Tarrytown, a character under the disguised name of John Anderson. He looked somewhat like a reduced gentleman. His small clothes were nankin, with long white top boots, in part, his undress military suit. His coat purple, with gold lace, worn somewhat threadbare, with a small-brimmed, tarnished beaver on his head. He wore his hair in a queue, with long, black band, and his clothes somewhat dirty. In this garb I took charge of him. After breakfast my barber came in to dress me—after which I requested *him* to undergo the same operation, which he did.

When the ribbon was taken from his hair, I observed it full of powder. This circumstance, with others that occurred, induced me to believe I had no ordinary person in charge.

He requested permission to take the bed while his shirt and small clothes could be washed. I told him that was needless, for a change was at his service, which he accepted.

We were close pent-up in a bed-room, with a guard at the door and the window. There was a spacious yard before the door which he desired he might be permitted to walk in with me.

I accordingly disposed of my guard in such manner as to prevent an escape. While walking together, he observed, he must make a confidant of somebody, and he knew not a more proper person than myself, as I had appeared to befriend a stranger in distress. After settling the point between ourselves, he told me who he was, and gave me a short account of himself from the time he was taken at St. Johns in 1775 to that time. He requested pen and ink, and wrote immediately to Gen. Washington, declaring who he was. About midnight the express returned with orders from Gen. Washington to Col. Sheldon to send Maj. André immediately to headquarters.

I started with him, and before I got to North Salem meeting-house met another express with a letter directed to the officer who had Maj. André in charge, and which letter directed a circuitous route to headquarters for fear of recapture, and gave an account of Arnold's desertion, etc., with directions to forward the letter to Col. Sheldon. I did so, and before I got to the end of my journey I was joined by Capt. Hoodgers first, and after by Maj. Talmadge and Capt. Rogers. Having given you this clew, I proceed with the Major's own story. He said he came up the North River in the sloop of war *Vultu*re on for the purpose of seeing a person by flag of truce. That was not, however, accomplished. Of course he had to come ashore in a skiff, and after he had done his business, the wind was so high, the Dutchman who took him ashore dared not venture to return him on board. The night following, the militia had lined the shore, so that no attempt would be made with safety. Consequently, he was furnished, after changing his clothes, with a Continental horse and Gen. Arnold's pass, and was to take a route by Peekskill, Crumpound, Pinesbridge, Sing Sing, Tarrytown, etc., to New York.

Nothing occurred to disturb him on his route until he arrived at the last place, except at Crumpound. He told me his hair stood erect and his heart was in his mouth on meeting Col. Samuel B. Webb of our army face to face. An acquaintance of his said that Col. Stoddert knew him, and he thought that he was gone, but they kept moving along and soon passed each other. He then thought himself past all danger, and while ruminating on his good luck and hair-breadth escapes he was assailed by three bushmen near Tarrytown, who ordered him to stand. He said to them: "I hope, gentlemen, you belong to the lower party." "We do," says one. "So do I," says he, "and by the token of this ring and key you will let me pass. I am a British officer on business of importance, and must not be detained." One gua.

of them took his watch from him and then ordered him to dismount.

The moment that was done, he found he was mistaken and he must shift his tone. He says, "I am happy, gentlemen, to find I am mistaken. You belong to the upper party and so do I, and to convince you of it, here is Gen. Arnold's pass," handing it to them. "Damn Arnold's pass," said they. "You said you were a British officer, where is your money?" "Gentlemen, I have none about me," he replied. "You are a British officer, with a gold watch and no money! Let us search him." They did so, but found none. Says one: "He has his money in his boots; let's have them off and see." They took off his boots, and there they found his papers, but no money. Then they examined his saddle, but found none. He said he saw they had such a thirst for money, he would put them in the way to get it if they would be directed by him. He asked them to name their sum to deliver him at Kingsbridge. They answered him in this way: "If we deliver you at Kingsbridge, we shall be sent to the sugar-house, and you will save your money." He says: "If you will not trust my honor, two of you may stay with me and one shall go with the letter I will write. Name your sum. The sum was agreed upon, but I cannot recollect if it was 500 or 1000 guineas, but the latter, I think, was the sum. They held a consultation

a considerable time, and finally they told him
if he wrote, a party would be sent out and
take them, and then they should all be prisoners. They said they had concluded to take
him to the commanding officer in the lines.
They did so and retained the watch until Gen.
Washington sent for them to Tappan, when
the watch was restored to Maj. André.

Thus, you see, had money been at command,
after the imprudent confession of Maj. André,
or any security given that the British would
have put confidence in, he might have passed
on to Sir Henry Clinton's headquarters with
all his papers and Arnold's pass into the bar-
gain. I do not recollect to have seen a true
statement of this business in any history that
has fallen into my hands.

There is something infinitely touching in
the relations of these two young officers. The
heart of the Lieutenant was warmed with pity
and sympathy for his captive, and no one can
doubt from this recital and from what afterwards transpired, that if honor had permitted
he would gladly have set him free. On the
other hand, the British officer, fully appreciat-
ing this sentiment and knowing that he was in
the keeping of a gentleman, gave no hint of a
readiness to purchase his liberty, as he had

openly done when he was dealing with the "bushmen."

The friendship thus begun under such painful circumstances grew stronger every day until the end of the sad story. The American Lieutenant accompanied the British Major to headquarters, passed days and nights with him in his prison chamber, walked with him to the gallows, and stood by him when he said: " I am reconciled to death, but not to the mode. It will be but a momentary pang," and then deliberately adjusted the rope to his neck with his own hands.

André was a spy ; Nathan Hale was a spy.

It requires more patriotism to be a spy than to serve in any other capacity in war.

Let England cherish the memory of her hero ; let us cherish the memory of ours.

Notwithstanding the verdict of history, which agrees with the declaration of Gen. King that "to the imprudence of the man, and not to the patriotism of any one, is to be ascribed the capture of Major André," the people of Tarrytown rightly determined that the spot of the transaction should not be forgotten. They could not very well erect a monument to chronicle the great event which

saved our country from unspeakable disaster,
without symbolizing it by the actors, to whatsoever motive at heart they might ascribe their
conduct.

For many years there had been standing by
the roadside in private grounds an unpreten-
tious little pyramid with a commemorative in-
scription upon it.

This was replaced in 1880 by a column of
larger size, surmounted by a bronze statue
representing one of the bushmen, musket in
hand, in an attitude like that of the picket
guard in the well-known statuette by Rogers.
It is artistic in all respects excepting that the
fingers of the hand held back in caution, are
so very long that no one can fail to be struck
by the want of proportion in this small particu-
lar which detracts from the merit of the work
as a whole. If Dr. Coutant would climb up
by means of a ladder and amputate a few
inches from each of those preposterous fingers,
his surgical skill would commend itself as
much as his antiquarian lore to our gratitude.

The topography of the country has somewhat changed since Irving made it the scene

of " The Legend of Sleepy Hollow." We are
told that

" In the centre of the road stood an enormous
tulip tree, which towered like a giant above all
the other trees of the neighborhood and
formed a kind of landmark. Its limbs were
gnarled and fantastic, large enough to form
trunks of other trees, twisting down almost to
the earth and rising again into the air. It was
connected with the tragical story of the unfortunate André, who had been taken prisoner
hard by, and was universally known by the
name of Major André's tree. . . . About 200
yards from the tree a small brook crossed the
road and ran into a marshy and thickly
wooded glen known by the name of Wiley's
swamp. A few rough logs, laid side by side
served for a bridge over this stream. On that
side of the road where the brook entered the
wood, a group of oaks and chestnuts, matted
thick with wild grape-vines, threw a cavernous
gloom over it. To pass this bridge was the
severest trial. It was at this identical spot
that the unfortunate André was captured, and,
under the covert of these chestnuts and pines
were the sturdy yeomen concealed who sur-
prised him. This has ever since been considered a haunted stream, and fearful are the feelings of the schoolboy who has to pass it alone
after dark. . . Just at this moment a plashy
tramp by the side of the bridge caught the sen-

sitive ear of Ichabod.   In the dark shadow of
the grove, on the margin of the brook, he be-
held something huge, misshapen, black, and
towering."

This brook no longer runs across the road,
but as the grade has been improved, it flows
through a culvert far beneath the present
level, and would scarcely be noticed by the
passing traveller.   Here it was that old Gunpowder took the bit in his teeth and pursued
his mad race side by side with the headless
horseman.   They   reached   the   road   which
turns off to Sleepy Hollow, but " Gunpowder,
who seemed possessed with a demon, instead
of keeping up it, made an opposite turn and
plunged headlong down hill to the left."

The tulip tree has long since disappeared,
the thick woods have been cut down, and
the marsh has been drained.   This downhill road has also been somewhat diverted
from its original line, but people who follow it
generally imagine that Sleepy Hollow is at its
base, and that the bridge crossing Pocantico
Creek is where the final catastrophe occurred.
But that is neither Sleepy Hollow nor the
bridge.   The house of Hans Van Ripper, with
whom Ichabod boarded, was in Sleepy Hollow,

higher up, on what is now the Bedford road.

There, also, was the old log school-house, since replaced by a building of more modern architecture. An old lady of the neighborhood perfectly remembers the original structure, " the windows partly glazed and partly patched with leaves of old copy-books." Farmer Van Tassel must have lived at a considerable distance south of Sleepy Hollow, as the pedagogue had found it necessary to borrow a horse for the occasion of the party. Old Van Ripper was well paid for the loan, for he made himself and Gunpowder immortal among the rest.

Thus we can trace nearly all the localities of the tale and yet agree with the cautious Mr. Knickerbocker in his comments upon it : " Still he thought the story a little on the extravagant ; there were one or two points on which he had his doubts." The old bridge, now taken away, was further up the stream, and the road has been somewhat changed accordingly. Therefore the headless horseman is no longer seen. He probably rode down to the brink one dark night, and, unaware of the removal, plunged into the stream, and rider and horse were drowned.

Fanny trotted as quietly over the new bridge as if none of these wonderful events had transpired a century ago.

A few rods beyond is the old church—not whitewashed now, but showing the gray color of the rock of which it is built. There are signs of some outward renovation, which do not detract materially from the appearance of age, and the little pepper-box belfry still contains the original bell, imported, with many of the inside fixtures, from Holland. On a tablet above the door we read, " Erected by Frederick Phillips and Catharine Van Cortlandt, his wife, 1699." It stands as an outpost on the southern wall of a great city of the dead, where its founders with successive generations of their tenants repose, and where later generations lie side by side with them, people who came to possess themselves of their land when living, against their will and protest, but who share it with them now in peace. The little bell called the first settlers together to worship God in the ritual and language of their mother church. Afterward the old Dutch liturgy was abandoned for more modern doctrines expressed in English. At last, for all practical purposes, there is no more service of any kind, excepting during the month of August, when the Antiquarian Society, whose property the building has become, open it for preaching, rather for purposes of curiosity than for devotion.

In this cemetery is the grave of Irving. When I visited it a few years ago and stood by the simple white slab on which is inscribed his name and the date of his birth and death, and saw that it was evidently new, I asked the keeper if it could be possible that all this time should have gone by with nothing to designate the spot. "Oh, no, indeed;" he replied, "a stone was put up almost immediately, but the curiosity-hunters chipped it to pieces, and this has taken its place. They will probably serve it in the same way and then there will be another."

And yet let us not too hastily accuse them of desecrating his grave. The stone was not broken down and strewed around with malicious intent. Each little bit may have been carried away with thoughtlessness, but with pious motive, and wherever it is, it may be cherished as a token sacred to his memory.

CHAPTER VI.

*Along the Tappaan Zee.—The Pathfinder's Home.
—The Old Van Cortlandt Manor-House.—
Up the Croton.—Two Views of the New
Dam.—Revolutionary Memories.—Canaan-
ites of the Seventeenth Century.*

THE old Albany Turnpike, as it is still sometimes called beyond Tarrytown, where I do
not remember having seen any more sign-
boards indicating that it is Broadway, is true
to its name for the intervening six miles before we reach Sing Sing, the country residence
of New York ex-Aldermen and ex-financiers
in general. They are there, solving the prob-
lem of capital and labor by equalization with
the horny-handed sons of toil who erstwhile
worked with revolvers, bowie-knives, and bur-
glars' tools.

The road is all "up hill and down dale,"
passing over eminences that command some
of the finest views of the Hudson where it

spreads itself out into the wide Tappaan Zee, forming a picturesque lake at the base of the opposite mountains. Notwithstanding the eligibility of the many commanding sites, fine mansions do not abound. It is somewhat too far from the great business mart for men to go to town every morning and return every afternoon. If the river be followed still further to the Highlands, where the scenery is most impressive, or to Poughkeepsie and even beyond, where it is still beautiful if not so wild, it will be found bordered at greater intervals either by mansions of retired gentry who go to spend the last years of their lives in the country, or by villas for merely summer occupation.

On this bit of turnpike stands a fine house once owned and occupied by a man now retired from public notice, but who in his day was one of the foremost characters of the country. "The Pathfinder" he was called in his youth, when, full of enthusiasm and love for adventure, he traversed the prairie deserts, discovered the Great Salt Lake beyond the Rocky Mountains, and led his band of avant couriers over the Sierras Nevadas down the slope to the Pacific shore. He was the first to unfurl the national flag in California, and to aid in founding a new empire in the West.

There he gained wealth and the honor which made him the Free-soil candidate for the Presidency. In the war of the Rebellion he was the pioneer of freedom, the first to declare, before he was justified by the progress of events, that the war was a struggle for the liberty of the slave. Here on the Hudson, in a paradise of forest and shrubbery, he established his home. Here he and "our Jessie," as the people delighted to call her, a woman whose attractions and commanding presence entitled her to the leadership of society in Washington, made their happy and luxurious dwelling-place, dispensing elegant hospitality, and surrounding themselves with the best and the most cultured of the land. Then misfortune came upon them. The great Mariposa grant of thousands of acres, exceeding dukedoms of the Old World, was wrenched from their hands, their lovely home was sacrificed and became the property of others, and they were almost thrown upon the charities of the world.

But are republics ungrateful? O, no, Frémont was rewarded in his old age for all that he had done for the nation. They made him Governor of Arizona, with a salary large enough for a small politician, and they went to live and to be buried alive in those hot and desert lands. Strange contrast this from their shaded lawns on the Hudson! They soon came back to the East, and are now—who knows where?—ending their days in obscurity and neglect. Thus passes the glory of the world. New heroes have come upon the stage and gone, and the Pathfinder, too, is dead, although he still lives.

Soon after passing through the village of Sing Sing, the post-road makes a sudden turn to the left, and spans the Croton River with a substantial bridge near its mouth. On the opposite bank stands the time-honored Van Cortlandt manor house, one of the most interesting relics of ancient days.

It was built by Stephanus Van Cortlandt, the first "lord of the manor," in 1681, the date as chronicled on the door-post at the entrance. It was evidently intended originally rather for a fortress than for a dwelling-house, the loopholes for musketry used against the Indians which indicate this, being still in such condition for defence that I have some-

times wondered that the present lady of the
manor does not bring them into use to ward
off the many strangers whose curiosity attracts
them to the spot. But that is not the dispo-
sition of the amiable and courtly hostess who
has so often entertained me and others at her
hospitable board. Proud she is, and well may
be, of the history of her late husband's ances-
try, of the portraits of the Van Cortlandts,
from the first Stephanus down to the present,
of their trophies and memorials, of the original charter from the crown, of wonderful
curios of plate and crockery, of the old home
itself, solidly built of bricks said to have been
brought from Holland, of its wainscoted
walls, huge fireplaces, venerable chairs, and
the dark mahogany table, around which ancient Dutchmen first made merry, and the
great generals of the Revolution afterwards
did justice to its cheer when Col. Philip Van
Cortlandt was the master of the house.

He himself was one of the bravest of the
brave, a man without fear and without re-
proach. His own incorruptibility led him to
suspect Benedict Arnold long before his treason, and in his journal he alludes in terms by
no means complimentary to him as appropriat-

ing the property of the Government to his own use. Familiar is the story of the attempt to bribe Ethan Allen, and of his reply to the offer of a large tract of land from the King. " It reminds me of the promise of the devil, on one occasion, to give away all the kingdoms of the earth, when the d——d rascal didn't own a foot of the ground." So, in the beginning of the war, according to the family chronicle, Gov. Tryon came up to Croton, and, inducing Van Cortlandt to walk with him to the top of the highest hill on his estate, promised him all the land in sight, and a title besides, if he would adhere to the royal cause. Tryon received, if possible, a more indignant reply, and hastily embarked upon his sloop to return to New York.

The old burgomaster, Oloff Stephense, the head of the family, has had no occasion to be ashamed of any of his posterity. He was the original settler, having landed in New Amsterdam in 1638. A thrifty old Dutchman he was, who instantly began to acquire property. But Stephanus, his first-born on this continent, was still more adventurous. He bought immense tracts of land from the Indians, and the colony soon afterwards coming under

British rule, he consolidated all his territory and obtained the royal charter, still carefully preserved, which created him the first lord of the manor. The area of his possessions extended from the Croton River twenty miles north, and from the Hudson east to the Connecticut line.

Mr. Henry George would have looked upon the ownership of so much land by one man as a heinous offence. According to his theory, the Indians, who had previously held it in common, must have been a happy and prosperous set of men. Nor would he have stopped to consider what was sure to be the distribution of it. Children were born, and children's children's inheritances divided and dismembered it, until to-day the possessor of the manor-house holds but 2000 acres, all the rest having gone into the hands of strangers. For one or two generations real and personal property may remain in a family, and then all is scattered, perhaps to be heaped up again by some one at the bottom who exchanges places with those who were at the top. Our philosopher would have it all equalized at once and kept forever on an equality. This scheme will be successful when the tides cease to ebb and flow, and when Nature, convinced of her error, throws down the Rocky Mountains and the Sierras to convert the ground into building lots and farms.

Mrs. Van Cortlandt, who is withal a lady of rare literary ability, is at present compiling a work which will be of great interest not only to the various branches of the family, but to the public in connection with their history. The participation of Westchester County in the events of the Revolutionary war will find a prominent place. On one of the proof-sheets we were permitted to see, we read an extract from a letter written by Pierre van Cortlandt, November 13, 1775, to his son, the Colonel: " Thursday night were here to supper and breakfast of Col. Hammond's regiment about three hundred men. They said they drank two hogsheads of cider." And doubtless there was a store of Madeira in the cellar for more distinguished guests. It is added, " Franklin tarried here on his way back from Canada in 1776. Here, too, came Lafayette, Rochambeau, and the Duke de Lauzun." Washington was here many times while the army lay on the shores of the Hudson and along the heights of the Croton. In more peaceful days the great

Whitefield had preached, standing on the broad veranda, to spell-bound crowds on the lawn, who had been summoned from miles around by horsemen sent out by Van Cortlandt.

All this pageant passed before me in a vision of the past, and then it was speedily dispelled as the shrill whistle of a passing locomotive echoed over the now quiet loneliness of the scene. Then, bidding adieu to the lady of the manor, I descended the steps over which the spurs of Revolutionary heroes had clanked more than a century ago, and mounted my horse from the block where they were accustomed to take their "stirrup-cup" to the health of their entertainers.

Turning off from the Hudson at this point, we now began to follow the Croton towards its source. The little river was "dark as winter in its flow," for the boulders covered with snow and with shining icy jewels made the water black by their contrast, and the recent freshet, which had not subsided, was playing wild music along the foamy channel. For miles, until we reached the lake beyond the present reservoir, the stream sparkled and danced in the sunlight of its winter glory.

But the end must come to everything, and although

> " Rivers to the ocean run,
>   Nor stay in all their course,"

the Croton will be one of the exceptions. Its happy days will soon pass away, and it will settle down to dull repose as a motionless lake. " A stagnant pond it will be," said Mr. Orlando Potter, whom I met in my travels.

"Well, Mr. Potter," I said, "you have fought till the end against the scheme, but its advocates have triumphed over you." "Yes," he replied, "but they have to contend against the Almighty now. First, they have to sink for a foundation 110 feet to a porous bed-rock that may let all the water out as fast as it runs in, and then the dam is to be 177 feet above the ground level, the water to flow back more than eight miles, and to spread itself from one to two miles up into the valleys. What a reservoir that will be for a little river like this to fill! What with the leakage and the evaporation, it cannot be kept full in hot weather. There will then be a slimy border of decomposed vegetation, breeding malaria around the country, and the putrid water will

also breed pestilence in the city.   If the job is
ever completed, $20,000,000 will not cover the
cost.   But that is the least consideration in
this terrible blunder."

Such was the opinion, and I doubt not the
sincere opinion, of the defeated general of the
pessimists.   On the other hand, a triumphant
optimist who, by the bye, would get rid of a
large tract of land, worth from $50 to $100
per acre for farming purposes, at a valuation of
$300, pitched his jubilate in the highest key.
" What a grand idea it was ! " he exclaimed.
" Now the city can spread itself indefinitely.
Ten million people will have all the water they
want, and then what a thing of beauty, what a
joy forever, this lovely sheet of water will be !
Ten miles long, indenting the shore with
charming little bays where the tall shadows of
the hills and trees will reflect themselves as in
the mirror lake of the Yosemite ; boulevards
all around this great expanse, country seats
with lawns sloping to the banks and—"

"But," I asked, interrupting him, " how
about the drainage from these houses ? "
" Oh," he replied, " that is the easiest thing in
the world to arrange.   Great mains with pipes
to cross the brooks can be laid along the

shores, and not a particle of pollution can enter the lake, as it will all be carried down below the dam."

Such are the differences of opinion which may be decided at some future day when the younger readers of these pages are gray-headed.

Turning from the river at Pine's Bridge, a locality made famous by the passage of André, we follow the road to Bedford. It is certain that André crossed this bridge. Nothing else pertaining to his exciting ride is more sure. That he landed at Verplanck's Point, and was afterwards captured at Tarrytown, is not more so, but he appears to have had so little topo-graphical knowledge, and was naturally so confused, that, in his narrative to Lieut. King, he could not give an exact account of his jour-ney. Historians have since duly lined it out and have given him a great many parallel roads to travel upon. If you ask any old farmer in Verplanck's, Peekskill, Shrub Oak, or York-town, about it, he will say that he has "hear'n tell that Andree passed directly by his house." It is at all events undeniable that he could not have reached Tarrytown without crossing this bridge unless he forded the river.

The people hereabouts are "champion liars" as to the events of the Revolution. This propensity of theirs has been serviceable in giving Fenimore Cooper many hints, which he has judiciously woven into a thread of fiction, more resembling truth than the alleged truths themselves. It was from a citizen of Bedford that he heard of one Enoch Crosby, who had the reputation of having been an American spy. Crosby grew into Harvey Birch, and Harvey Birch became a reality.

War began at an early day on the borders of New York and Connecticut, long before the Revolutionary struggle in which the battles of White Plains and Ridgefield were fought. The Dutch and the English entertained the same views of the Indian question that are prevalent among their descendants. The latter gave for the land all along Long Island Sound, extending sixteen miles inland, twelve coats, twelve hoes, twelve hatchets, twelve glasses, twelve knives, two kettles, and five fathoms of wampum. There was a treaty "reserving the liberty of hunting and fishing for the Indians."

But our ancestors came to loggerheads with the Indians on the "fishery question," as we are now embroiled with the Canadians. They, too, passed measures of retaliation, not paper measures, like those of Congress, but measures of powder and ball, such as our down-East smack owners would like to have the nation pass on their account against Canada. The result of the fight in 1644 was very satisfactory. One hundred and thirty troops, most of them Dutch, under Capt. John Underhill, exterminated 700 " savages," first setting their village on fire and then driving men, women, and children back into the flames. It is mentioned by the historian as a proof of the incorrigible obstinacy of these people that they perished without uttering a single cry. But, like the Israelites of old, the Dutch considered that God was present on the occasion to help them, for " the Lord collected most of our enemies there to celebrate some peculiar festival."

There is now a Quaker meeting-house hard by the spot of that inhuman massacre. This peaceful sect came here too late for the poor Indians. There was no William Penn among those cruel Dutch to stay their hand, and to inculcate the policy of peace by which he obtained his conquests, and which gave to Pennsylvania the true title-deeds for her lands,

while those of New York and New England
were written in blood.

The Indians having been exterminated, the
white men who became possessors of the soil
occupied it by right of might, as the Jews occupied Canaan after the destruction of the
Amorites, the Hittites, the Jebusites, and
other similar savages who had been smitten by
"the sword of the Lord and of Gideon."
Then their own turn likewise came to be massacred or carried into captivity—and they
thought it hard. So the people of Bedford
failed to appreciate the retribution which, we
are told by the highest authority, descends
upon later generations for the sins of their
fathers, when, in 1779, Tarleton swooped down
upon them and burned their town. The
neighborhood was the scene of many skir-
mishes during the Revolutionary war, and in
most of them the patriots, though far exceeding the British in numbers, were defeated, not
so much because of their cowardice as for want
of arms and discipline. But what Bedford
lacked in military skill it compensated the
country for in giving birth to the greatest dip-
lomat of the time. In that capacity John

Jay was of more account than regiments of soldiers or parks of artillery.

Night was closing in upon us again. Fanny and I on a roundabout road had already accomplished thirty miles. Ten miles beyond, over the Connecticut line, lay the village of Ridgefield to which we hastened on. Again from another domestic hearth the cheerful wood fire gleamed, and again I was welcomed to the house of my old schoolmate and friend.

> " I praise the Frenchman, his remark was shrewd,
> How sweet, how passing sweet, is solitude ;
> Yet grant me still a friend in my retreat
> Whom I may whisper, solitude is sweet.
>
> " Hast thou a friend ? Thou hast indeed
>   A rich and large supply ;
> Treasure to serve your every need,
>   Well managed, till you die."

Yes, it is very pleasant to have "a rich and large supply" of friends along the road.

CHAPTER VII.

New York as a Summer Residence. — The Country in Winter. — The Old Boston Post-Road. — On the Way again to Ridgefield.

THE thermometer is not always an indicator of temperature. That depends quite as much upon the quantity of moisture in the atmosphere as upon conditions that are frequently only apparent. In the high altitudes of the West we are less uncomfortable in our shirt-sleeves with the mercury at zero than we find ourselves in New York when wrapped in flannels and ulsters, the glass showing thirty degrees.

Another atmospheric peculiarity we cannot fail to notice. Directly upon the seashore the climate, whether the thermometer corresponds or not, is milder than it is ten or a dozen miles inland. Thus, as Brighton and Hastings afford relief from the bitter winter winds of London, so Atlantic City and Long Branch have become refuges from New York, and the value of Coney Island in this respect will ere long be appreciated.

Undoubtedly people become acclimated to New York, and find its temperature, as well as everything else that really makes it attractive, the best in the world. But these are they who never go away from their home, and who consequently never experience any inconvenience in returning to it. Perhaps, after all, they are more contented than vagrants who wander all over the world in search of happiness because they fancy that on Manhattan, where it could easiest be attained, the air does not agree with them. Nevertheless, it must be admitted that there is at least "a change of air" experienced by going either to the seashore or to the country in winter as well as in summer. Indeed, if I were compelled to divide the time by seasons between city and country, I would unhesitatingly give the summer to the former and the winter to the latter.

I would like to be a millionaire so that I
could buy up and pull down the old rookeries
which were once the chosen abodes of New
York merchants, on State Street, but are now
converted into immigrant boarding-houses and
tenements, and build dwelling houses in their
stead.   I fancy that it would be a good
investment.   What more can a quietly disposed family desire than a house comfortable at all seasons, one which in the summer
looks out on the green lawns and trees about
Castle Garden, where the sultry winds of July
and August are tempered and refrigerated by
their passage over the salt waters of the bay
and the rivers?   There, perhaps, at no very
distant day, residents of the New York that is
to be above the Harlem will find their summer
homes, when Trinity Church shall stand alone
in its rural cemetery and the fragments of
Wall Street may come into use for fencing the
lawns sloping to the river banks and the
market-gardens along the sides of Broadway.
There will then be no question of getting out
of New York.   New York will get out of itself.
The Harlem River will be its southern boun-
dary, and it will stretch away to the north,
with the new Croton Lake, ten miles long and

three miles wide, for its centre, and its upper limit will be somewhere near where I am now writing, on the shores of Lake Mohegan.

I look upon it this lovely February morning from my window, its surface covered with a sparkling field of new-fallen snow, the pines and firs surrounding it bending under the white plumage so beautifully contrasting with their green, the oaks and maples with frosted barks and silver icicles glittering in the sunlight. This is winter, glorious winter. It quickens the pulse of age and brings back the memories of youth, the jingling bells, the rosy cheeks, the ringing laughter of the sleigh-ride of the olden time, the music of the gliding skates—all the wholesome, life-giving exercise in its pure, bracing air; and still to me it is more joyous than the gentle zephyrs and balmy airs, green landscapes and tropical verdure of the South, that boasts of its sunny clime, but where never sun shone with a splendor like this of to-day.

The story of "The Pioneers" opens with a charming winter scene, depicted with the graphic pencil of nature that Cooper always held in his hand. The keen atmosphere makes our blood tingle, and we luxuriate before the

blazing logs in imagination as if we had partic-
ipated in their warmth.   The winds are as cold
now on the banks of the Otsego, but the music
of the bells is not so merry, for fashion has
decreed a noiseless gliding over the snow, and
the cheerful fireside has given place to abom-
inable stoves, furnaces, and steam-heaters.

In the early days of our history, winter
sports were more appreciated because there
was so little sport of any kind.   The business
of life was serious.   The minds of our fathers
were occupied mainly with the questions how
should they get a living in this life by works,
and how by faith they should make sure of a
life to come.   Since their day, the struggle for
existence has become less arduous.   Wealth,
bringing luxury, has poured in upon their descendants ; the rough edges of religion have
been smoothed off ; and shocking as the idea
would have been to their ancestors, men have
determined to get out of it all the enjoyment
which the world can afford.   Some of the
morning newspapers find space for reports of
sermons on Monday, but on every other day
of the week their columns are filled with the
particulars of horse and yacht races, base-ball
and foot-ball games.   These, for the most part,

are summer sports, but now is the season for "carnivals," ice-boating, skating, sleigh-riding, and tobogganing, the most healthy and invigorating of them all. Perhaps, by and by, as autumn excursions on horseback have lately become popular, the same delightful exercise may be taken in winter, the season of all seasons which I have found from oft-repeated experience to be for it the most enjoyable.

It is now 1888. We parted company a year ago at Ridgefield, Conn., and if you please we will start again from there. Fanny and I have since that time borne each other's burdens. She has carried me often over many roads, and I have paid her stable bills. Her appearance still denotes content, and she never gives me any cause of complaint, excepting that on the approach of a railroad engine she manifests fear, and turns about, trotting away from it till its noise subsides.

It is a female characteristic to be afraid of something. A steam engine is as objectionable to a mare as a cow or a mouse is to a woman. We should make due allowance for this imperfection in the house or in the stable. If Fanny could speak, she would doubtless find some weak point in my character. I am glad that she cannot. We do not like to be told of our faults.

As I am unable to persuade any human friend to accompany me on my long rides, our companionship becomes closer. Fanny knows the pocket in which I keep the lumps of sugar. When she gets one of these little dainties, she acknowledges it by a cordial shake of hoof and hand. She knows perfectly well whether we are about to take a long or a short journey, for in the first case I always show her the small roll of baggage before it is buckled upon the saddle. So she adapts her gait to the requirements of the trip. We talk together along the road—that is to say, I talk to her and she listens. Many people think this is the best way to carry on a conversation. It is not uncommon, and it always affords pleasure to one person at least. By this means the rider may place himself *en rapport* with his horse. There is no exact English for this French term. It means a great deal—not precisely that a man is any part of a horse, or that a horse is any part of a man, but that the man for the time being is equine, and the horse is human in his feelings.

To the saying of Terence that because he

was a man nothing human could be foreign to him, I would add that for the same reason nothing about a horse can be foreign to me. I believe that a horse has a soul. The Bible tells us that there are horses in heaven, and that they came down from thence to take up Elijah. I think that even bad men get to heaven at last, and there is no reason why horses, who are better than they are, should not get there before them. Several years ago this question of the immortality of animals was discussed in the columns of the New York *Evening Post.* It was shown that many men of very sound minds believed in it—prophets and apostles of old, like Isaiah and John the Revelator ; later theologians, like Martin Luther, and scientists like Cuvier and Agassiz.

It matters not how we found ourselves at Ridgefield again, so far as the description of the road is concerned. The town is easy of access by the old Boston Post-road through White Plains and Bedford, fifty-three miles from New York. Fanny and I have often travelled over it, and I have called to her attention the few remaining mile-stones and the tumble-down aspect of old farm-houses long

9

since deserted. I might have asked her, and
obtained an answer as satisfactory as I can get
from others or from myself, how it is that the
farmers hereabouts and the farmers of New
York State and New England manage to live.

When these large houses were occupied,
their inhabitants did live by raising produce for
the city markets before railroads were known.

According to the theory of the protectionists, they should live better now by supplying
the factory establishments which have been
built up in their neighborhood. But stubborn
facts may disprove any economic theory. The
farmer's occupation for everything but the
sale of milk is gone. The articles that he once
sold he is obliged now to buy. Even his hay
sometimes comes from the West. His land is
not worth the half of its price of fifty years
ago ; and yet, although he acts in direct opposition to the scheme of Senator Frye, who
counsels us to sell everything and buy nothing
if we desire to be successful, he does live
as he did not live in the olden time, when he
and his family wore homespun dresses, when
he worked, his wife worked, his sons and
daughters worked, and when he had nothing
but hard-wood furniture and rag carpets.

Now, his boys, if they have not "gone into business," drive fast horses, his girls wear seal-skin sacks and silk dresses, make music with the piano instead of with milk pans and butter churns, and they all live in a new nicely-furnished house and have plenty of money. How is that Fanny? Fanny shook her head, by which I understood that, with all her horse sense, she could not fathom it. "I can't see," I continued, "how the farmer can be so prosperous when he not only sells nothing, but buys everything, and that at a high price, in order to support home industries, which give him nothing in return. I think I'll ask the philosopher of the *Tribune.*" Fanny tossed her head. I did not exactly understand if this was in token of approbation or contempt; but when I added, "He will probably attribute it to the beneficent tariff," she snorted outright. I saw that she was thinking of oats, and wondering how, if the price should be advanced from forty-three to sixty cents per bushel, either she or I would be benefited.

CHAPTER VIII.

Ridgefield to Danbury.—The Burning of the Town in 1777.—The Battle and Other Revolutionary Incidents.

THE mercury stood at six degrees above zero in the morning at Ridgefield. It had rained on the previous day, and now the sun shone as it shines here through a foliage and over a landscape of glittering silver. Indoors the prospect was as satisfactory as it was charming without. The cheerful fire in the breakfast-room, the aroma of the coffee, the juicy steak, the frequent relays of buckwheat cakes that came upon the table hot from the griddle, and the mug of hard cider which always goes with a genuine country breakfast—above all, the society of my hospitable entertainers—were strong inducements for delay. But the *vis inertiæ* of the after breakfast easy-chair was at length overcome, and wrapping my stirrups with straw, pulling

132

the blanket back over my legs in the manner
heretofore described, and drawing my cap
down over my ears, I was ready to start on
the road to Danbury.

It was over many hills which the rain of the
previous day, now become ice and covering
the snow, had adapted to the purpose of
toboggan sliding rather than to that of riding, unless horseshoes are exceptionally well
sharpened. Under these circumstances the
rider who supposes himself very careful is
apt to walk his horse slowly over the ground,
especially when descending hills. That is an
easily demonstrated mistake, for a little reflection must convince him that the animal
should be put to a hard gallop so that the
shoe corks may strike heavily and effectively
into the ice. The necessity for doing this
caused the distance of ten miles to be overcome in little more than an hour, and that
was the end of the day's journey, for before
our arrival the clouds had gathered and the
snow had begun to drive in our faces after the
manner, though in a milder degree, of a Mon-
tana blizzard.

It was a harder road to travel for the British troops 111 years ago. From Mr. Bailey,

the witty editor of the Danbury *News*, who can be serious occasionally, and who in one of his serious moods has done good service in writing some interesting historical sketches, I obtained more information than I can compress into this chapter, pertaining to the events of the Revolutionary war.

To go back to the time when Danbury was a mere protoplasm, existing under the Indian name of Pahquioque, it was bought from the natives and honestly paid for in trinkets, blankets, and rum by some adventurous Yankees who had found their way from the New England coast first to the valley of the Connecticut, and thence had come as near as they dared to approach to their former enemies, the Dutchmen, here establishing an outpost in 1684. They underwent the usual experiences of border warfare, being often alarmed by the demonstrations of the Indians, but never having any serious conflicts, perhaps because they were always in a condition of defence.

But a small area of the Connecticut valley was then occupied, and it is therefore difficult to imagine any motive but that of Puritan aggressiveness that could lead them to institute a war against nature in this rugged coun-

try when the rich and easily explored river
valley lay open before them, a hundred miles
to the north and a hundred miles to the south.
The Puritans were like the Irishman who
always wants somebody to tread on the tail of
his coat, and like Mark Tapley who was
happy only when he was miserable. For mutual protection this devoted band lived in
block-houses together, and from them they
went out four or five miles every day to cultivate the best soil they could find. After
they had escaped all danger from the Indians,
there came the French war to disturb but not
to injure them. Their real suffering came at
last in the war of the Revolution, when nearly
the whole town was destroyed and the earn-
ings of a century were annihilated by the
flames in a single day.

In April, 1777, Gov. Tryon came from New
York with 2,000 men, and landing from their
boats at Fairfield, they marched to Danbury
for the purpose of destroying a considerable
quantity of Continental stores that had there
been collected. These were "guarded by a
few Continental troops without arms." So
the American story runs, and it is added that
on the approach of the British, they " with-

drew." It would not have been to their discredit if the truth had been told that they ran away, although it was to the discredit of somebody that valuable property like this was so totally unprotected.

The British entered the town on the night of April 26, and immediately burned one house with four persons in it, and on the next day set the whole town on fire. They destroyed about 5,000 barrels of salted provisions, 1,000 barrels of flour, 1,600 tents, and a quantity of rum, wine, rice, etc. Besides these the estimated private losses were over $80,000.

The American and British accounts of this conflagration differ only in the use of adverbs. The American report says: "The town was wantonly burned." The British report says: "The town was unavoidably burned." Thus we see on what slender threads hangs the truth of all history. For the credit of humanity it may be said in corroboration of Gov. Tryon's story, that on their march through Bethel, where there were no munitions of war, private property was unmolested.

In Danbury almost the only buildings spared were the Episcopal church and the tavern. The former owed its safety to the regard of the pious Tryon for the established religion of his country, and the latter to the presence of mind of Mrs. Taylor, the landlady. When the soldiers were about to apply the torch she had a large batch of dough ready for the oven. "Why, boys," said the comely matron, placing her arms akimbo, and looking smilingly in their faces, "I was just going to bake some nice biscuits. If you burn the house down, you'll lose your breakfasts ; if you don't, you'll see what good bread a Yankee woman can make ; and I guess I can find some rum to go with it. The old man has run away, but I've got the key, and I'm no more afraid of you than you are afraid of me. Sit down and make yourselves comfortable till breakfast is ready." The soldiers took her at her word. She "kissed them all for their mothers," they had a good breakfast, and went on their way rejoicing. Taylor's tavern stood for many years, a monument of the ready wit of Taylor's wife.

The oven figures once more in the history of Danbury. Eli Benedict and Stephen Jarvis were the Tory pilots who led the enemy into the town. They both "withdrew" to Nova Scotia, to await the issue of the war.

If the British had been victorious, they might
have returned to become office-holders, but as
things turned out it was the part of discretion
to stay away. Benedict never came home,
but Jarvis, after many years, had an irrepres-
sible desire to visit his friends. He came to
them in disguise, but his presence in the town
was suspected. The mob came to the house
of his sister where he was imperfectly concealed. Again a woman's fertility of resource
came into play. She pushed her brother into
the great brick oven, and piling him over with
kindling-wood, bade the intruders search the
house ; and they searched it in vain.

On the first appearance of the British, ex-
presses were sent to Gens. Arnold and Wooster at New Haven. They arrived one day too
late for effective service. If they could in
season have collected even a few men, they
might have swept down on their enemies at
night, when they lay around the smoking
ruins of the town in the stupor of intoxication.
They arrived, however, on the next day, and
dividing their forces, Arnold pushed on ahead
over the road I had just travelled, to fortify
a pass against the enemy's approach, while
Wooster followed in their rear.

Without being a military critic, it appears to me that Wooster was too precipitate. He should have allowed the British to come up against Arnold's defences, and thus brought them between two fires. Instead of adopting such cautious tactics, he pursued them impetuously, so that, although they were not in a fighting mood, but only anxious to secure their retreat, they faced about and whipped this detachment of the Continentals, mortally wounding Gen. Wooster in the engagement.

Turning about again, they came up with Gen. Arnold, whose small force was unable to stop them unaided by the assistance that Arnold had counted upon, although he and his men resisted courageously till all hope was lost. The British then made their way through Ridgefield to their boats, harassed but not seriously impeded by sharpshooters, who peppered them as opportunity offered.

As usual, American and British accounts differ enormously as to the number of killed and wounded on their respective sides; but the desolation of Danbury bore witness to the fact that the object of the raid had been accomplished. Gen. Wooster was brought back to one of the few houses remaining, and died there two or three days after the action. The Congress at Philadelphia passed becoming resolutions and appropriated a sum of money for the erection of a monument to his memory. It is an almost incredible story that the amount being handed over to the General's son, who was authorized to exercise his own taste and judgment, he diverted the appropriation to his own uses, and left his father's grave without even a stone to designate its locality. A later generation has been more grateful to him than his unnatural offspring, and now a handsome monument records the heroic self-sacrifice of this intrepid officer.

It would have been better for the fame of Arnold had he, too, met his death upon this early battle-field. But he lived to display again and again his reckless courage in subsequent contests for liberty. No one can doubt that until his fatal step into the abyss of infamy he was actuated by the patriotism as much as by the ambition of a soldier. It was when the latter was disappointed that the former was betrayed. Like Lucifer, he fell from the stars, and as Lucifer's good deeds in heaven from all eternity are not remembered as a balance of account with his transgression, so all that Benedict Arnold ever did for the freedom of his country has been blotted out by his futile attempt to accomplish its ruin.

I sat for hours that evening in his library with the editor, who is an encyclopædia of historical knowledge, collating what I have written from his store of facts and anecdotes. As I was about to leave, he observed, " I am afraid you will have a cold ride to-morrow, but it is not as cold as it was Sunday morning. See that water-color painting? Looks damaged, don't it? Well, that happened Saturday night because there was no fire in the furnace. The water in the color froze." When I came to know Danbury better on the next day, I wondered why the paintings there were not done in whiskey: but my suspicions were now aroused by this remark of the jocular newspaper chief, and I asked, " Mr. Bailey, is this all true that you have been telling me? "

"True as Gospel," he replied, solemnly. " Do you believe the Gospel? " I inquired. " In the main," responded the editor. " Well, then," I answered, "I'll believe this in the main, for I know there was a Revolutionary war and I think it quite likely there was a fire in Danbury, possibly about that time. Good

night.   Many thanks." "Good night, call
again," and I was out in the street wading
through the snow to the Wooster House,
where I turned into a comfortable bed and
dreamed of British invaders mingled with
American patriots, and while there was a blaze
of fire all around, we were sitting in Mrs. Taylor's kitchen watching her as she baked hot
rolls for us, the British Generals Agnew and
Erskine, with Wooster and Arnold, drinking
healths to each and the other in Jamaica rum.

CHAPTER IX.

The Iconoclasts of Danbury and of Boston.—Hat Industry.—Storms on Sea and Land.—Ride to Mohegan.—Ice-Cutting and "Microbats" by the Way.

ON the next morning there was a driving snow-storm, but in this compact town it was not difficult to get about the streets. Some one pointed out the old church, which, as has been narrated, the British spared from regard to its religious denomination. They were more generous than the posterity of its occupants, who might have been supposed to have had sufficient veneration for it to maintain it in repair, and to perpetuate it for its original purposes. Instead of doing so they have sold it with less compunction and excuse than Esau had in disposing of his birthright. They were more hungry for show than he was for pottage, and so, as the building was not adapted to modern religious style, they sold it to be

143

moved away and to be occupied as a tenement house.

"I wish," said the late Harvey D. Parker, the proprietor of the hotel in Boston that bears his name, "they'd pull down that old King's Chapel opposite. Such kind of buildings ain't no use in these times." And then he turned around and viewed complacently the composite architecture of his feeding and lodging establishment. No one knows how long the venerable structure will be spared. Even in æsthetic Boston its continued existence is but a question of short time. Brattle Street church fell at the demand of fashion, and although the Old South was rescued by private subscription from the destruction to which its walls had been doomed by greed and religious ambition aided by legal chicanery, it has been robbed of its sacred character and has become a museum of curiosities, while its former occupants have taken the many times thirty pieces of silver for which it was sold, and which it had gained by more than two centuries of freedom from taxation, and built what they call "a magnificent church edifice," where it will be of benefit to the real estate that they own. The people of Danbury are not more iconoclastic than the Bostonians.

Mr. Hull, a merchant of the town, kindly piloted me into one of the large hat factories, where some idea might be obtained of the prevailing local industry. In this one alone 300 men and women are employed. Altogether, out of a population of 18,000, 3,500 men and 1,500 women are engaged in the various processes of making hats, in the twenty-four factories. They earn large wages, but the business is not regular and steady. In the latter part of the winter, and in early spring, "times are lively" in meeting the demand for summer fashions, and at the close of summer and the commencement of autumn the workmen are called upon to prepare for the requirements of winter. Six months' work in the year is about all that can be counted on. Although in "slack times" there is a scattering for a while into the country, and into the city of New York, there is necessarily a great deal of lamentable idleness. But there are always bright days for the rumsellers. They "toil not, neither do they spin." Others have done that for them, and they live much better than lilies of the field. In some of the streets al-

10

most every other house is a "saloon." In White Street, about 300 yards long, there are thirty-two of them. These are mostly patronized by the foreigners.

In former times the hat-makers were all Americans, and as machinery had not been introduced to any extent, they found an abundance of work. Even now, when less than half are Americans, the country boys and girls earn substantial wages, which, to the disgust of the saloon-owners, they keep for themselves. Near the factories are rows of sheds. Early in the morning caravans of wagons or sleighs may be seen coming into town, each vehicle carrying, besides its passengers, a bundle of hay. They drive to the sheds, where the animals are left to feed till evening, the boys and girls taking their dinner-pails along to their places of work. The days are long, for "piece-work" is indifferent to eight-hour rules. The busy employés reserve only light enough to find their way home, and at twilight they take up their line of march.

It seems to me that honest, industrious persons like these should have some very fixed and correct ideas upon "the protection of American labor." It may be supposed that

they would look askance on the introduction
of so much machinery, although they know it
is unavoidable, and now that they see half of
the remaining work, the whole of which was
once their own, being done by imported labor-
ers, they should ask themselves, "What is
the meaning of the hackneyed phrase? Is protection of machinery and of foreigners a protection of American labor, or is it the protection
of men who employ machinery, Americans,
foreigners, horses, mules, as they can best employ anything and everything for their greatest
advantage?"

Hats of all kinds have been made at Danbury. Just now, as the Derby hat is almost
universally worn, the stock and machinery are
adapted to its manufacture. If the "stove-
pipe" ever again gets the ascendency, new
methods will doubtless be devised. On entering the factory we were shown first the material out of which the hats are made. This
is mostly rabbit fur, and singularly the article
is chiefly imported, the greater part of the supply coming from Germany. One would suppose the rabbit industry to be indigenous, and
whatever protection sheep wool might require,
rabbit wool would need none. But the duty

on hatters' furs of twenty per cent. is often escaped by importing the free skins and stripping them here. I wonder if the Australians, know anything about Danbury and Derby hats? Rabbits are overrunning their country and devouring their substance. Why not trap a few millions of them, kill them, and send their skins to Danbury?

First we were shown cases of boxes, in each division of which from 2½ to 4 ounces of fur had been carefuly weighed out according to the weight of the hats intended to be made.

This is soaked and steamed in rooms of a temperature like that of a Russian bath, until it becomes pulp. Then it is spread with almost transparent thinness over a cone three feet high and a foot in diameter. Next it is shrunk and partially dried. By and by, after being dyed, it comes down to the size of an ordinary hat when it is blocked. Now it would answer for a " wide awake," but it must be stiffened with gum shellac and the edges curled. Thus far all this heavy and dirty labor has been done by men, each one having his piecework. At this stage it is turned over to the deft manipulation of the women, who bind, stitch, line, and pack. Then the carpenter comes and nails up the cases, and the hats are ready for shipment. I have enumerated only a few of the more than twenty processes of hat-making, each of which is the piece-work of separate individuals—all "parts of one stupendous whole." I don't know if that phrase is exactly applicable to a man's hat. It certainly is to that of a woman as regarded between ourselves and the foot-lights.

The relations between the factory-owners and their employés just now are amicable, but as among the great European Powers, war is not unlikely to break out at any moment. The workmen are masters of the situation. They know, as well as their employers know, to a penny what it costs to make a hat and what price hats command in the market. It is not the employer who fixes the wages of the employed, but it is the employed who figures out exactly how much the employer shall be permitted to make. The employés are all union men, and they will not allow a single non-unionist to work, nor will they permit any boy under seventeen, or man over twenty-one years of age to learn the trade. At present they are earning from three to five dollars per day, according to their capacity. That gives the

men who employ them a fair margin of profit.
If the market should advance, the workmen
will doubtless demand more, and if it should
recede, I think they are sensible enough to be
willing to take less rather than be idle. Danbury appears to have solved the great question
of capital and labor.

Every old sailor knows that a southeasterly
gale is most likely to expend its fury and to be
succeeded by a brisk nor'wester either at eight
o'clock in the evening, at midnight, or at noon.
When coming on to the coast, appearances are
closely watched at these hours. If there
should be a sudden lull, then is the time without a moment's delay to haul up the courses
and to stand by the braces. In an instant the
head sails are taken aback, and a lively crew
will swing around the after yards. The main-
topsail fills, and as the ship's head pays off, the
head yards in their turn are swung, and the
ship lies close to the wind, which comes rushing back from the cold north-west.

When this change occurs at noon, there cannot be anything more grand and beautiful than
the scene. The clouds of snow or rain that had
been driving everything before them in their
fury, are driven back upon themselves and

piled together over the eastern horizon by the young giant that has come out of the north scattering them with the breath of his nostrils. Every moment, his fury increases. After the southeaster has succumbed, its waves for a time keep up the uneven contest until the nor'wester brings into action the waves that he has created, and which increase under his lash. These strike the old seas and topple them up on end, sending the spray of the combat high in the air, little rainbows playing through their crests. At last the old leaden colored seas subside and the blue waters roll on in their beauty and majesty. The ship that had been tossed about in the conflict, opposing surges meeting and tumbling in upon her decks, is now snugly hove to, riding the billows like an albatross, and sailors, disappointed as they may be at the loss of their fair wind, are never so insensible that they cannot enjoy the magnificence of this great picture of sky and sea.

There is nothing comparable to it on the land. There are the same clouds, storms, and sunshine, the same poetry of motion overhead, but no motion of the stolid mountains that stand still in their everlasting ranges, fixed

there by the Power that gives to the mountain
waves their ceaseless moving energy of life.
And yet, if we cannot have the sea all the
time, let us be grateful for what the land affords
that is beautiful, if not so grand. The snow
cannot lie and sparkle on the breast of the
ocean, and there are no silver forests there—no,
nor sleigh-bells, toboggan-slides, and skating-
ponds, but, taking it all in all, leaving the
waves out of the account, could there be anything more superb than the breaking of the
storm that day at Danbury?

True to its propensity, this came about
precisely at noon, and the north-west wind
succeeded. As Fanny and I left the town at
one o'clock, the sleigh tracks were covered with
a dry powdered snow, which here and there
was whirled up against the fences, arching itself
over them in drifts and festoons. Everything
looked so white, so pure, so clean, as if there
could never be a thaw, when the roads would
become dirty brown, then black bare ground,
the barn-yards reservoirs of filth, the fences
naked and wet, and there would be "water,
water everywhere." I did not think of that at
the time.

There are many persons who would not have

enjoyed the present surroundings so much—the same sort of people who in health are always on the lookout for sickness, and who seem to be afraid to live because at some time or another they will die. There is where a horse generally has the advantage over a man. Horses probably have no idea of death. It might be a satisfaction to car horses if they had, but I do not think it would be a pleasant thought for Fanny. She gets her oats regularly, and, though the time may come when the oats are musty or are not, she doesn't trouble herself with anticipating evil. Let us all try to imitate her. She was in remarkably good spirits to-day. Facing the wind, the steam from her nostrils blowing back upon her face, she was a pretty and unique picture, with her bay body and legs and her silver-gray head. Sometimes a little stray forgotten snow-cloud would come travelling back from the west on its airy journey to overtake the storm that had left it behind. And then for a while we were all white till the wind had blown off the flakes. So cheerily we made our way along through Brewster's and Carmel until we came to Lake Mahopac.

Sad was the appearance of its great summer hotels, with their closed shutters and barricaded doors, huge snowdrifts piled upon the piazzas, the abandoned photograph shanties, and the boat-houses with their signs still displayed, " Boats to let "—boats to let, with ice eighteen inches thick, and a thickness of eighteen inches of snow over the ice.

But there was no lack of activity on the lake. Gangs of men were busily employed in filling the two great ice-houses, which hold 60,000 tons. Canals, nearly a quarter of a mile long, had been cut out into deep water so that the purest ice might be obtained. The great cakes were pushed along by men until they reached the shore, when a sort of steam tread-mill apparatus seized them and jerked them up to a high platform, from whence they slid down to lie side by side or one above the other in a compact mass until they were wanted for refrigerators, fever hospitals, ice-creams, mint juleps, and the thousand uses to which ice is put in summer, the most common and the worst of which is that of ruining the digestion of persons who drink ice-water with their meals.

There was not always such a craze for ice-water in this country. It has not yet invaded Europe. Doubtless it was to Mr. Breslin one of the most objectionable practices of the

London hotels that they do not serve goblets of this pernicious drink to their guests. I remember reading in an old magazine—I think of about 1802—an account of the tubing from a very cold spring near the "city prison" in New York, and it was mentioned as an especial advantage for those who lived at a considerable distance, that as the water had so far to run in the logs, "it lost somewhat of its coldness as when first taken from the spring."

I stopped to talk with a man who appeared to be directing some others at the lake, and congratulated him on the successful harvest of the crop. "Jes' so, jes' so," he said. "Well, yes, it will be a big thing this year—our folks can get any price they want."

"How is that?" I asked.

"Why, on account of them microbats in the North River ice. It's all pizen, and nobody will use it. Ours hasn't got any of 'em in it."

"Well, what's the matter with the North River ice?"

"Microbats, didn't I tell you! You get a microscope and examine a drop of that water: there's ten million microbats in it, and every one of 'em is a snake. They lay so clost to-gether that they keep 'emselves warm, and don't freeze when the water freezes solid. Then when the ice thaws out, there they be. Folks that drink that kind of ice-water get typhoid fever, malaria, measles, and small-pox, to say nothin' of having live critters crawlin' round inside of 'em."

"But how would they work in whiskey?" I suggested. "Wouldn't that kill them?"

"Now, that's something I hadn't thought of," replied the ice man. "Perhaps it might."

"Well, then," I replied, as I touched Fanny lightly with the spur, "New Yorkers, on the whole, may consider themselves safe."

Nine miles more to Mohegan, arriving at our old quarters there at five o'clock.

"Delightful ride, wasn't it, Fanny? I hope you are not tired?"

"Not a bit of it. Where are we going next?"

"I can't say just now. Here, take this lump of sugar, give me your paw, and trot off to your stable."

CHAPTER XI.

The West Side of the Hudson.—The Discoverer's Dream.—Revolutionary Memories.—On André's Track.—Over the Ice-Bridge.—Fanny's Misgivings.

FREQUENTLY passing up and down the eastern bank of the Hudson River, whether by rail or over the highway, the steep Palisades and the range of which they form a part, stretching far north to the higher Kaaterskills on the western side, in their varied dresses of the seasons, changing from green to russet-gray, and then to the silver of the frozen torrents or the dazzling white of midwinter, are ever-present pictures of scenery which familiarity cannot render tame or uninteresting. They seem to have been built up to hide something beyond and to excite our imagination with conjectures of what it may be. As Irving looked upon them from the porch of Sunnyside, he peopled them with the beings of his own fancy, turning loose his hobgoblins to disport themselves with a mortal who dared to trust himself in their wild recesses. Familiar as he was with that little strip of New York, which, to look at it on the map, would seem to belong of right to New England, and of which he could speak with accuracy, as he did in his "Legend of Sleepy Hollow," he was obliged to confine himself to imagination in his description of the terra incognita that he dared not to cross the river to survey.

There must have always been something forbidding about that western shore, for when Hendrik Hudson anchored in the river on the 11th of September, in the year 1609, he made no attempt to land upon it, but pulled away to an island on the other side, armed with a demijohn of gin, with which he attacked and subdued the natives, who, not having had any name for the spot, called it Manhattan—the place of drunkenness—in honor of the occasion ; and the name is still appropriately retained. In this first encounter with the aborigines, the harder and more accustomed head of the explorer stood him in good stead, although his share of the fire-water

may, perhaps, account for his prophetic dream
of the night.

The southern breeze had died away,
　　The ebbing tide to seaward ran ;
It was the twilight hour of day,
　　E'er night her starry reign began.

Hendrik had dropped his anchor there,
　　Beneath the bristling Palisade,
When sunset streamed its golden hair,
　　On Nature's face in slumber laid.

And as he paced the decks alone,
　　Fond memory brightened into hope ;
The past was his, and the unknown
　　Was in the future's horoscope.

He stopped, and gazing at the view,
　　Sat leaning o'er the galliot's side,
And saw the Indians' light canoe
　　Dance o'er the sparkling starlit tide.

The music of the parted stream,
　　The wafted land-breeze vesper sigh,
Stole o'er his senses, and his dream
　　Encouraged by the lullaby

He thought he saw the small canoe
  Grow big, and bigger—bigger yet,
Then changing into something new,
  It was a sloop with mainsail set.

And then this white bird had her young,
  They grew like her, and clustered 'round,
And " Yo heave ho " was cheer'ly sung
  As sloops were up and downward bound.

And still they grew, as Fashion's dames
  Increase in flounce and furbelow;
Brigs, ships, and craft of various names
  Float 'round the anchored Dutchman's bow.

'Twas nothing strange, he'd seen them oft,
  Perhaps less jaunty, snug and trim;
But then those flags he saw aloft,
  Those stars and stripes, were new to him.

But now he sees, or thinks he sees,
  A mill afloat, with water wheels
Revolving, coming near! His knees
  Shake with the fear that o'er him steals.

It thunders on with furious blast;
  It is the devil's ship of fire;
Like lightning sweeps the phantom past
  On bickering wheels that never tire.

Then underneath the lurid light
    She leaves above her foamy track,
Upsprings to his astonished sight
    A city on Manhattan's back.

'Tis pandemonium! Demons scream
    Through thousand whistles in his ear,
And fiends on iron horses seem
    To shoot along their mad career!

Through the still air, the midnight bell
    Sent out the music of its stroke ;
The anchor watch sang out, " All's well,"
    And Hendrik from his dream awoke.

To-day the crests of the Palisades are densely wooded as they were two hundred and seventy-nine years ago, and it is not till the traveller has progressed some twenty miles to the north that, looking across, he sees scattered houses, towns, and village cities that have crept down and established themselves on the waterside. People of the eastern shore do not care to have any intercourse with them. Before the Revolutionary war there was Dobbs Ferry above Yonkers, and King's Ferry above Sing Sing, but latterly there has been no cross-

ing-place below West Point excepting between
Tarrytown and Nyack, and the ferry-boat
which did that service having been burned, it
has not been thought worth while to replace
her.

About the line between New York and New
Jersey over there, there are curious old Dutch
settlements, and there are Revolutionary leg-
ends of battles and of the rank treason hatched
upon their shores. I have always desired to
tread upon their ground.

An opportunity was offered by the building
of the great natural bridge which this year has
stretched across the Hudson from its source
far down to within fifteen miles of New York.
How well the Ice King does his architectural
work! First he fringes the shores and spreads
his glassy outworks towards the channel; it
is a long time before they meet, but when
they touch and come together, the building
goes rapidly on, the substrata thicken inch by
inch until what seems to be the maximum of
two feet is gained.

In the last winter Fanny and I had gone
over the road travelled by the hapless André
from his landing on the eastern shore until he
was captured at Tarrytown, and his subsequent

fortunes were traced as he was led from place to place, a prisoner.   I now proposed to avail ourselves of the chance offered by the closing of the river, to cross it as near as might be, in an opposite direction, on the route of the old ferry which served André's purpose, for it is not true, as is generally supposed, that he was brought over by a row-boat in the darkness, being supplied with a horse after landing.

It was very cold on the morning of the 16th of February.   The mercury at eight o'clock stood at five degrees below zero, but the air was perfectly still, so that at ten, when the glass indicated zero, the lack of wind aided by the sun-warmth already appreciable in the advance of the season, rendered riding not only far from uncomfortable, but gave it a zest and enjoyment not to be attained under any other conditions.

Leaving Lake Mohegan we pursued our noiseless way over the well-beaten sleigh tracks, down through the village of Peekskill, meeting here and there a muffled pedestrian. Most of the people were occupied in the many stove foundries which contribute to its principal industry.   On a day like this they might well make themselves comfortable about their

stoves, and wish, for the success of their business, that all the days of the year might be
like unto it.

I once asked a stove manufacturer why he
was a protectionist, and why he so cheerfully
submitted to a heavy duty on the iron that
he worked. "Oh, well," said the manufacturer,
whose house had just divided the year's profit
of $48,000, "we can stand it ; we get enough
out of the public, and so we can afford to let
the pig-iron men get something out of us."
I did not propose just now to leave Fanny out
in the cold while I went into his office to argue
the question with him. She might have stood
there till this time, and my friend would not
have satisfied me that any reduction of the
duty on pig-iron would infallibly reduce his
own profits and the wages of his men.

Verplanck's Point, where it projects into the
Hudson, is four miles below Peekskill, almost
directly opposite Stony Point upon the other
side. The British held these commanding
positions, which gave them control of the
river. Later in the war they were abandoned,
and the Americans extended their lines nomi-
nally to the vicinity of Tarrytown, although
the intervening ten or fifteen miles were at

times included in that debatable terriority in-
fested by Cowboys and Skinners, and known
as the "neutral ground."

The fortress on Stony Point was captured
in July, 1779, by Gen. Wayne, with the aid
of the first "intelligent contraband" on rec-
ord. Old Pomp had supplied the British garrison with strawberries, and in the routine of
his business he became possessed of the coun-
tersign. The primary attack of the Americans
was upon Pompey's cabin, where he was captured and subdued with little difficulty. At
first he refused to betray his customers, but
by dint of promises of many chickens and
threats of disabling his shins, he was induced
to lead the Continentals into the stronghold.
Wayne advanced by the side of Pompey at
the head of his troops under cover of darkness,
and after a hand-to-hand bayonet fight, without firing a single gun, they subdued the
garrison and took 543 prisoners. In the end,
after being evacuated and again occupied by
the British, the forts on both sides of the river
were abandoned and dismantled, the King's
Ferry being continued between the points.

Fanny and I approached the river at the
spot in Verplanck's where André landed under

the guidance of Joshua Hett Smith, who fig-
ured conspicuously in the treason, and to
whose connection with it I shall give a prominent place in this narrative, because his name
has not always been brought forward with
those of his principals. The river, frozen with
a thickness of nearly two feet, was still further
covered by a foot of snow. Far as the eye
could reach to the Highlands of the north,
and beyond the wide Tappaan Zee at the
South, it was all an unbroken prairie of white.

We might have crossed in the exact track
of André and Smith to Stony Point, a distance of about a mile, but by taking a diag-
onal course of four miles to Haverstraw there
was a saving of time. To all appearance
a great field lay before us. Why should
Fanny suppose it to be anything else? She
had never been there before. Why should
she know that beneath that fair covering of
snow there was a layer of ice, and that beneath
the ice there was water enough to drown a
thousand regiments of cavalry? There was
not the slightest difference in the look of the
snow upon the river and upon the land over
which we came to it. Nevertheless, she was
so reluctant to follow the foot-tracks that I

was obliged to dismount and give her a "stern board." Even then, when once upon the river, she trembled excessively, and looking into her eye I could see the thought in her brain, and knew that if she could speak she would say: "I have every confidence in you, but I am a female and you must make allowance for me. You say the ice is two feet thick; but I might break in. Can't we go around by the bridge at Albany or the ferry at New York? No? 'Come on, Fanny, is it?' That's all well enough for you. You say you will lead me till I gain more confidence; but these are tracks of men. Horses weigh a great deal more than men, and I don't see a single horse-track on the snow!" Caresses and sugar, however, had some effect, but she stepped timidly and gingerly along until we came to the well marked sleigh-track. All at once her fears vanished as she trod it with a firm step, and permitting me to mount her, she loped over the frozen river as if it had been a highway upon the land. Animal instinct, was it? No; it was thought, reflection, calculation, like that of a man, without his knowledge of safety— nervousness, fear, distrust, like that of a woman, which refuses to be overcome by reason.

So we went on confidently and satisfactorily until suddenly there came one of those, to the inexperienced, fearful ice-quakes, giving the impression that our weight was cracking and breaking down the great winter-bridge through all its length and breadth, and that we were about to sink into the depths below. The hills on either side took up the echo, and poor Fanny thought that her last moment had come, and that she was about to expire in a convulsion of nature. She stood still and trembled from head to foot. Cold as it was, the sweat broke out upon her, and with it the hair on her skin literally stood on end. I never so pitied a dumbthinking beast. Dismounting, I put my arm around her neck, drew her head down to my breast, patted her face, and kissed her cheek, yes, I did, and I walked by her side comforting her as best I could for the rest of the way, as again and again the fearful, though harmless, crashes reverberated from shore to shore. For her sake, I was glad when we landed at Haverstraw.

CHAPTER XII.

The " Smith House" at Haverstraw.—A Revo-
lutionary Copperhead.—The Landing from
the " Vulture."—Two Fateful Musket Shots.
—The Cider-Mill Engagement.—Smith's
Misadventure.

I HAD a letter of introduction to Mr. Lilburn, who, I had been told, had lived in the
" Smith house " for many years, and who now
resided in the new house that he had built
near by. We had crossed the river, landing
two miles below the place, but Fanny was so
overjoyed at being on terra firma again, that
she skipped nimbly over the road to find an
entertainment as agreeable to her in Mr. Lilburn's stable, as was provided for me at his
hospitable board.

The events of the Arnold treason are narrated in books of history, and are often repeated in magazines and newspapers. Never-

theless, there are items to be gathered on the
spot, brought down by tradition, seasoned perhaps with romance, but having for their stock
the meat of truth.

After dinner, my obliging host accompanied
me to the historic house, where we were politely received by Mr. and Mrs. Weiant, the
present occupants.   It cannot be agreeable to
the privacy of family life to dwell in a " show
place."   No one would care to live in Shaks-
pere's home, or at Mount Vernon, if they could
be had house-rent free.   But these kind people
declare that they are not disturbed by their
frequent visitors, who are always made welcome to explore the premises.

The house was built 140 years ago.   It is
one of those old-fashioned structures whose
builders studied architectural comfort rather
than architectural monstrosities of " kitty-cor-
nered " roofs, mediæval turrets, and all sorts of
composite irregularities that are laid to the
charge of good Queen Anne.   On each side of
the wide hall, with its ample staircase, are two
large square rooms, duplicated by similar
chambers overhead.   The first chamber in the
south-east corner is the one where Arnold and
André were closeted and where the plans of

West Point were delivered. A part of the original furniture is still there. A little secret closet is pointed out where André was said to have been concealed; but this is one of the absurd traditions which, I believe, Lossing has adopted as authentic without reflection. There can be no foundation for it whatever, as there was no pretence of secrecy in his visit to the house.

Mr. Smith was a gentleman of high social standing and wealth, but his great mistake lay in his abortive attempt to sit comfortably on two stools, which finally brought him ignominiously to the floor. He was a sort of Revolutionary Copperhead. As he intimates in his little book, copies of which are very rare (but one of them is in the possession of Mr. Lilburn), published in England and reprinted in America after the war, he was a Tory.

In those days there were Tories of two classes. The out-and-out Tory was one who stood by the King through thick and thin, opposing the war as unjustifiable from the beginning, and maintaining his allegiance squarely by taking up arms in the cause of his sovereign. The other was the man who acknowledged the grievances of the colonies, but was opposed to their separation from the mother country. When England, alarmed at the negotiations which resulted in the alliance with France, manifested a willingness to accede to the original demands of the colonies, the Tories of this stamp supposed that all the objects of the war might be accomplished, and therefore objected to its continuance for the sake of a distinct government, which they conceived would be for the interest of military and political agitators, among whom they classed Washington himself.

It may be added that there was still a third class who, like the old woman whose husband was fighting with the bear, " didn't care which whipped," so that she was not disturbed. All that they were anxious about was the safety of their own lives and property. For the first class we may well entertain a sincere respect. Certainly our Republican friends, who consider taxation for the benefit of the few to be an advantage to the whole community, will agree with them that it was a wicked thing for anybody to war against the King of England because he endeavored to collect a small duty on tea ; and all of us are willing to accord to sincerity in error something of the credit due to principle.

In his treatise, Mr. Joshua Hett Smith declares that he was on the American side, although he thought the war had gone far enough, while facts show that he was not only destitute of all patriotism, but was supremely selfish, and what was infinitely worse, he connived at the betrayal of his country.

To all indications, when the British lines extended above Haverstraw, he was a loyal subject of the king; but when his property came within the American lines, he lavishly extended his hospitalities to the Continental officers. Arnold and Burr were frequently his guests, and the latter left his name carved in the marble of the dining-room mantelpiece, where it is shown as one of the curiosities of the house.

In his book, Smith complains that he was not taken into Arnold's confidence, regretting that he was therefore unable to defeat his plans, while he unconsciously makes it evident that he knew perfectly well the object of André's visit, assisting in his disguise by lending him his own coat. It was this reluctant exchange of his uniform which settled the

British officer's doom as a spy, and Smith,
together with Arnold who proposed it, were
responsible for his fate. It is curious to notice how the case was regarded by some jour-
nals in England. The (London) *Political
Magazine* of February, 1781, says of it:
"Washington has tried Smith for being in
what they call Arnold's conspiracy; but the
trial has turned out a mere farce, for Smith
has not suffered any punishment. The people
in New York therefore believe that Smith betrayed André to the rebels, and are of opinion
that he never can clear up his character anywhere but at the gallows!" Truly the way of
the transgressor is hard. If Washington could
have convicted him, he would have hanged
him, and if the editor of the *Political Magazine*
had gotten him in his power, he would have
had him hanged again. He escaped the first
execution before his trial was concluded, by
disguising himself in women's clothes and getting down to New York, where fortunately for
him, Sir Henry Clinton did not take the edito-
rial view of his case.

The *Vulture* had anchored off Croton Point,
not far below Haverstraw, and Arnold at
Smith's house had furnished him with a flag of

truce to communicate with her. It was rather odd that a boat carrying such a flag should have approached the ship with muffled oars by night, and it is not surprising that the bearer met with a rough reception from the officer of the deck. It was with difficulty that he gained admittance to Capt. Southerland's cabin, and presented his credentials. Maj. André, under the name of John Anderson, then accompanied him to the shore, where they landed just below Haverstraw, and found Arnold concealed in the bushes, while a servant was in charge of two horses. Here was the first conference, in which Smith complains that he was not allowed to participate. It was prolonged till daylight when, the tide not serving for André's return to the ship, he and Arnold mounted the horses and rode through the town to Smith's house, while the latter pulled around with the boat's crew to an upper landing, with the intention of rowing André down to the *Vulture* on the turn of the tide.

In the meantime important events were occurring on the opposite shore, small in their beginning, but of infinite importance in results. But for them André would have effected his escape safely, Arnold's plans would have matured, West Point would have fallen, British communication with Canada would have been opened, the war would have been brought to a close, and these United States might have remained till this day the colonies of Great Britain. All this was prevented by two musket shots fired from a cider-mill.

On the morning of September 22, Moses Sherwood and Jack Peterson, a mulatto who afterwards enlisted in the army and received a pension for his services, were working their cider-press at Croton Point, on the farm which of late has been known as Underhill's vineyard. As was customary in those stirring days, the men carried with them their muskets to their places of work or of worship. These two had watched the movements of the English man-o'-war with suspicion, wondering what her errand could be, so far from her usual anchorage.

Their suspicions were increased when they saw a boat put off from the *Vulture*, possibly with the purpose of communicating with the western shore to discover the cause of Maj. André's delay. Each took up his musket, and one after the other fired upon the boat, the last shot splintering an oar, and causing an immediate return to the ship, which forthwith entered into a spirited engagement with the cider-mill. The noise brought all the neighboring farmers to the spot, and as fortunately there was a twelve-pounder field-piece at hand, it was brought into requisition. They dragged it down to the end of the point and directed it over a bank of natural earthworks against the *Vulture.* She replied with round shot, one of which lodged in an oak tree. When the tree fell from decay not many years ago, the ball was extracted, and is now one of the many curiosities gathered by Dr. Coutant at Tarrytown. The farmers made it too hot for the sloop of war, and she accordingly dropped down the river, out of range.

The conspirators at Haverstraw had witnessed the action, and, as may be imagined, were chagrined at its consequences. Smith himself was too badly frightened to undertake the return of André by passing the battery and running the risk of being overhauled by patrol boats, and as Arnold was unaccountably unwilling to provide another flag of truce, the boat's crew became suspicious and absolutely refused to go upon the errand. Arnold accordingly departed for his quarters, after providing Smith and André each with a pass, and instructing the former to escort the latter to a place of safety, whence he might find his way to New York.

Dr. Coutant has the facsimile of André's pass from Arnold. It is written with a steady hand on a bit of paper about the size of a half page of a note sheet. Late in the afternoon Smith and André mounted the two saddle-horses that had been used in the morning, and rode three or four miles up the river to the ferry at Stony Point. The horses were taken across with them in the scow which served for the King's Ferry transit. Thus the landing at Verplanck's Point was effected, but as yet the spy and the traitor did not feel at ease.

Smith was a good pilot. After finding comfortable lodgings at the house of McKoy, a Tory Scotchman, on the Yorktown road which was taken in order to avoid the American militia scattered along the river bank, they went on in the morning to Pine's Bridge, where they parted, Smith directing André to take the road through to White Plains, and thus avoid the river altogether. Last winter Fanny and I traced them along this road and came to the corner below Pine's Bridge, where André, left to his own resources, made his mistake of turning to the right in the direction of the Hudson. Smith pursued his route, not homewards, but towards Fishkill, where his wife happened to be, congratulating himself on his perfect safety after so many hairbreadth escapes, for they had twice been called upon to show their passes on the road, and once narrowly escaped detection. He jogged along comfortably and arrived at Fishkill in due time.

But he was a greatly astonished man, when, after the conscientious discharge of his patriotic duties, sleeping by the side of the partner of his previous joys and future sorrows, he was roughly dragged from his bed and taken down to Washington's headquarters, at what is now Garrison's Landing. He could not understand it at all. But he was soon brought to " a realizing sense of his lost condition."

I wonder that no historic painter has portrayed that meeting of Washington and Joshua Hett Smith. Smith coolly asked the General why he desired to see him, and why the invitation to his presence had been so rude and abrupt. He had not long to wait for the

answer. "Sir! Do you know that Arnold
has fled, and that Mr. Anderson, whom you
have piloted through our lines, proves to be
Maj. John André, the Adjutant-General of the
British Army, now our prisoner? I expect
him here under a guard of one hundred horse,
to meet his fate as a spy, and unless you confess who were your accomplices, I shall sus-
pend you both on yonder tree before the
door!"

Even then, Smith's audacity did not forsake
him. He says that he undertook to "argue
the question" with Washington, informing
him that he was exceeding the limits of his
authority, and that he should demand a trial
before the civil court, for he was not under his
command in the army. "Whereupon," he
adds, "the General was irritated and ordered
the guards to take me away." It is said that
on rare occasions the Father of his Country
supplemented his discourse with expletives.
If ever they were justifiable, the occasion for
them was when this impudent scoundrel was
before him.

CHAPTER XII.

*The First Battle in American Naval History.
—Over the West Shore Ridges.—The Old
Village of Tappan.—André Memories and
Relics.*

I LEFT my kind-hearted host, Mr. Lilburn,
returning many thanks for his hospitality, for
the information imparted by the documents
in his library, and the supply of traditionary
lore at his command. Fanny, too, was re-
freshed, for the oats served out to her were
not musty, like the papers I had feasted upon.
Evening was drawing on, and we had a ride
of twenty miles before us to Piermont, where
I proposed to pass the night with a friend, one
of those sensible men who believe that the
city is the place for business, and the country
is the place for home where clubs, theatres,
and the demands of society add not to the
toil of the counting-room, thus making life an
ever revolving tread-mill, on which rest is
never found.

Riding again through the town of Haver-straw, and following for a few miles further along the bank of the river, I think of more Revolutionary incidents than I have space to chronicle. All the way from Nyack to Haver-straw, wherever a landing could be found, the British made their incessant raids. Had the people been united, few and scattered as they were, these incursions would have been of less account. In our late sectional war we were geographically divided, and for the most part States were open adversaries of States, but in that of the old days no man could tell if his next-door neighbor was his friend or his enemy.

Far greater atrocities were perpetrated by Tory townsmen on the patriots among whom they dwelt, with whom they professed friend-ship and worshipped God, than by the invad-ing British troops. It is not surprising that when the war was over, the property of the Tories was confiscated, and they themselves were driven into exile. In the ancient local histories we read of assassinations and brutali-ties almost incredible, occurring in this region of the country settled by quiet Dutchmen, surpassing in enormity anything of their nature in all other parts of the land. From the Ramapo Valley to the shores of the Hudson there were constant successions of murder, rape, and arson. Patrols were always on guard to prevent the landing of the British, not so much from fear of them as from the apprehension that their own townsmen would be encouraged by their presence to cut their throats.

Exasperated by these frequent occurrences, they organized an impromptu fleet for the purpose of attack upon the water. Although it does not come within the scope of the great works on American naval history to chronicle it, nevertheless the first naval battle after the Declaration of Independence was fought directly opposite the road upon which I was now riding. On August 3, 1776, Skipper Ben Tupper constituted himself the first Admiral of our Navy, and with a fleet of four sloops, attacked the British ships *Phenix* and *Rose*, fighting them for two hours, and finally driving them below Tarrytown, within their own lines. This action was followed by a series of similar engagements to ward off the hostilities that for the most part were directed against the people of the western shore while the inhabitants on the opposite side of the river were comparatively unmolested.

Two or three miles below Haverstraw the boldness of the shore makes a road impracticable. We turned to the right, following up a steep hill that was to bring us over to the other side of the river coast range. It leads through a gorge, which in summer must be most attractive to the many tourists who come from the city to saunter in the shade of its trees and rocks. The trees, naked in winter, are clothed with verdure in the summer, but the rocky cliffs through which the road is cut, bare as they are in summer, were now draped in silver sheen and fringed with icy stalactites.

Before we left the level, the shadows of the hills had fallen over the frost-bound river, but now that we had mounted to the summit we caught up with the bright light and saw far in the west over that hitherto undiscovered country, the snow-clad hills and valleys, the black forest, the straggling towns and villages, a wide-spread panorama of surprising beauty, just as the last touch was being given to it by the setting sun. Then we descended the western slope and went rapidly on a few

miles more through the valley until we came
to another pass of the hills, through which we
reached again the river bank at Nyack. It was
a beautiful moonlight night, tempting to the
merry sleigh-riders we met constantly as we
passed through the town and its suburbs till
we came to the house of my friend in the out-
skirts of Piermont.

In my travels about the world I have frequently had occasion to contrast the habits,
manners, and social characteristics of its different peoples. I have never gone among any,
civilized or uncivilized, who were absolutely
inhospitable. The savage is often as hospitable as the Christian. I will not switch off
from my track so far from the main route of
this narrative as would be necessary to tell the
story of a three months' entertainment by an
Eastern Rajah, which would go far to establish the universality of this charming domestic
virtue.

I cannot help it if the careless reader shall
accuse us of being "dead beats" along the
road. I sometimes think that we are. Nevertheless, if we are asked to come again, we shall
go, for I have arrived at the conclusion that
there is no more genuine and sincere hospital-

ity in the world than among our own countrymen, and that they never pass the Spanish
compliment of placing everything at your
disposal without meaning it to be strictly
true that the house is your own for the time
being. I found it so at Piermont, and Fanny
found the stable exceedingly to her liking, as
was demonstrated by her activity on the following day.

I had in years gone by wandered with my
host through vineyards and under the shade
of the olive trees of the Mediterranean Isles,
and now I found him seated by the side of
his " fruitful vine, with his own olive-plants
around his table." Then it was burning summer, now it was " frosty yet kindly " winter.
There it was sunshine without. Here it was
sunshine within.

On the next morning the weather had mod-
erated so that although the ice and the snow
still maintained their grip, the sun heat was
preparing them for a speedy dissolution, and
the icicles, the roofs and the trees began to
drop tears in view of their coming departure.
The road again turns inland, passing down-
wards several miles behind the Palisade range.

On arrival at Tappan, a distance of four

miles, I called upon the minister of the village
church, and presenting a note from my host of
the previous night, was cordially welcomed at
the parsonage. It is one of those old-fashioned
Dutch houses—Mr. Williamson could not tell
exactly how old—that was built in the first
part of the last century, if not even earlier, a
solid structure of thick stone walls, large chimneys, low-studded with heavy cross-beams. I
fancy that on the library table, which like all
the furniture including the big clock that has
ticked with slow measured cadence dealing
out their spans of life to the many succeeding
dominies but still as youthful itself as the
jolly sun upon its face, there have been vol-
umes of sermons written in Dutch for the edi-
fication of the crumbling bones and dust now
in the venerable churchyard. Half a century ago Dutch was continued as the pulpit
language of many churches in south-western
New York and north-eastern New Jersey.
Latterly these Dutch churches have been
"Reformed" in language and doctrine, so
that, although they have come to differ
in no essential degree from Presbyterians, they
retain their former name only out of regard
to the old associations connected with it.

Fanny went to take her ease in a stable that had been occupied by more generations of horses, than the house had held of men, now dead and gone, the first of which may have been a square-built galliot-shaped animal, imported from Holland. Then, the dominie having shown the yellow church records and other curiosities of his library, took me upon a walk, discoursing as we went on incidents of history, and particularly of those concerning the last days of Major André.

The church in which his trial was held, was built in 1694, rebuilt in 1788, and replaced by the present structure in 1835 at a gain in size, but as would appear from the drawings, at a loss in architectural taste. The same remark may apply to the quaint stone-built Dutch house occupied by Washington as his head-quarters, but now, although its main part is left standing, disfigured by the addition of a flat-topped wooden wing after the modern style of Jersey renaissance. The present occupant unfortunately had gone away with the keys in his pocket, so that we could only survey the exterior; but Mr. Williamson pointed out the corner room where, when the procession passed on the way to the gallows, Wash-

ington sat with the curtains drawn, commun-
ing with his own thoughts, and wishing from
his inmost soul that the bitter cup might
have passed from the unfortunate victim.
And yet it was a woman, who only lacked the
claws and the fangs of a tigress, who assailed
him thus:

"Oh, Washington! I thought thee great and good,
Nor knew thy Nero thirst of guiltless blood!
Severe to use the power that Fortune gave,
Thou cool determined murderer of the brave!
Lost to each fairer virtue that inspires
The genuine fervor of the patriot fires!
And you, the base abettors of the doom
That sunk his blooming honors in the tomb,
The opprobrious tomb your hardened hearts decreed,
While all he asked was as the brave to bleed!
Nor other boon the glorious youth implored
Save the cold mercy of the warrior sword!
O dark and pitiless! Your impious hate
O'erwhelmed the hero in the ruffian's fate!
Stopt with the felon cord the rosy breath,
And venomed with disgrace the darts of death!
Remorseless Washington! the day shall come
Of deep repentance for this barbarous doom!
When injured André's memory shall inspire
A kindling army with resistless fire.
Each falchion sharpens that the Britons wield,
And lead their fiercest lion to the field!
Then, when each hope of thine shall set in night,
When dubious dread and unavailing flight

Impel your host, thy guilt-upbraided soul
Shall wish untouched the sacred life you stole,
And when thy heart appalled, and vanquished pride
Shall vainly ask the mercy they denied,
With horror shalt thou meet the fate they gave,
Nor pity gild the darkness of thy grave!
For infamy, with livid hand shall shed
Eternal mildew on thy ruthless head!"

The author, Miss Seward, was the friend of Honora Sneyd, who had discarded André, and had since married and died. That appears to be all of the personal motive which brought out this vindictive curse upon the head of Washington.

Nearly opposite the house occupied by Washington is another stone building of smaller size. It was a tavern in Revolutionary times, and for the occasion, a room in it was used as André's prison. It is now the property of an eccentric old physician, who has allowed the roof to tumble in and everything to fall out of repair. Lest any visitor should put one of the granite blocks or one of the roof timbers in his pocket and walk away with it, the doctor has surrounded the house with a high board fence which even the agile school-boy is unable to surmount.

We walked from the village in a westerly

direction over the road travelled by André to
his doom on the 2d of October, 108 years ago.
Of the Court of Inquiry of six Major-Generals
and eight Brigadier-Generals that found him
guilty and deserving of execution, Gen. Steuben
was the only one who was disposed to be
lenient, while Gen. Parsons, who manifested
no mercy for him whatever, was ten months
afterwards discovered in correspondence with
Sir Henry Clinton, with a view of betraying
the Continental Army.

What a sad farewell it must have been to
this beautiful world for one so young, before
whom there was everything that we old men
have left behind—for pleasant as retrospect
may be, some clouds hang over it ; but antici-
pation has not one dark spot upon it to dim its
brightness. It was the most delightful season
of the whole year, at high noon, when from the
hill on which he stood he could see the country far and near, clothed in all its glorious
autumn array—the yellow fields lately reaped,
the green pine forests, the already changing
maples in their parti-colored dress. There
stood the crowd around him who were yet to
live and yet to have these scenes before them,
who were still to inhale the balmy air of which

in a moment more he should breathe the last;
and harder than all he was to die an ignomin-
ious death with the fear that its baseness would
ever attach to his memory. Who would not
have pitied him, and what man could there
have been in that assembly who would not
have rejoiced to have seen him go free if the
traitor Arnold could have been made to suffer
in his stead?

A touching tribute to his memory, written by
Dean Stanley on his visit to the spot, was en-
graved on the monument lately erected there
by one of our countrymen, but it was soon
destroyed by some persons who were actuated
by personal malice more than by patriotic zeal.

CHAPTER XIII.

Through Bergen County.—Two Revolutionary Scenes.—André's Prophetic Lines.—A Lonely Inn.—The Dutch Landlord and His Family. —Return to New York.

PARTING from the amiable clergyman of Tappan with a high appreciation of his kindness, I mounted Fanny again and crossed immediately over the border line which separates Rockland County of New York from Bergen County of New Jersey. Schraalenberg was the first village to which we came after a ride of six miles, the country becoming more distinctly Dutch as we progressed. There were numerous quaint old stone houses, many of them with huge projecting stone chimneys, these denoting the highest antiquity when the great industry of Haverstraw and Croton had not been exploited. It has been said that the early settlers imported their bricks from Holland, but I apprehend that this legend refers

to ornamental tiles rather than to building
material. Of these many were brought over,
and to this day they may be seen bordering
the great fireplaces, where for generations the
catechisms and texts of instruction painted
upon them have served the purpose of the
modern Sunday-school. There, too, are still
the barns modelled like Noah's Ark bottom up,
low studded like the houses, for as land was
cheaper than it now is in Broadway, the heavy-
moulded farmers did not care to stretch their
legs needlessly in going up-stairs or to weary
their arms in pitching hay.

Everything but the landscape resembles
Holland. That is in all its aspects totally
different, for Bergen County, at least in its
northern part, is not spread over a level, but
runs from one hilltop to another. In South
Bergen, where there are plenty of swamps, the
Dutchman might have felt at home, but on his
first coming here he must indeed have considered himself a pilgrim in a strange land. How
did he get here, anyway? Did he climb over
the Palisades, or did he drift with the tide up
the Hackensack? What was he to do without
canals? I have noticed that in Java, where
there are salubrious hills and mountains easily

accessible, he deliberately established himself on the morass at Batavia, so that he could dig a canal, and then die of the yellow fever contentedly.

Why, indeed, did he not settle on the Hackensack meadows? Why do not his countrymen come there now? The descendants of men who redeemed Holland from the sea could surely rescue these meadows from the encroachment of the Hackensack and Passaic Rivers. There is room enough there for a thousand farmers of holdings such as they cultivate with so much success at home. The land is as good and the climate as equable ; but it is a waste, a great area of bog. We may imagine it the property of a thousand sturdy Dutch farmers who have not yet been corrupted with our air of liberty and broken out with the eruptions of extravagance and discontent. We see in our fancy the dykes thrown up and the intersecting canals on which the noiseless *trekschuit* glides along, the scattered houses and barns, the church spires and windmills, the long avenues of trees, the orchards, gardens, and fields, all possessed by a contented people. They could not live so cheaply here as in Holland? Per-

haps not in all respects just now; but a
change is coming. Still, will anybody tell us
why a colony of Dutchmen, who are not am-
bitious for luxuries they have not at home,
and who would have a better market for their
products than they have there, could not
thrive under these conditions?

I do not think that the higher altitudes they
sought in their settlement here, improved the
temper of the colonists. From all accounts
they became very quarrelsome in theology and
politics. When the Revolutionary war came,
neighbor was pitted against neighbor even
more ferociously than were their countrymen
on the banks of the Hudson. But they were
always a hard-working economical set of
people. They made home industries pay.
Everything they consumed, with the sole exception of the indispensable gin, was produced
by themselves. Men, women and children
worked in the fields, and even the baby's
weight was utilized in churning butter.

Their descendants to-day, among whom
their language and customs prevail more or
less, are not in the least intimidated by the
threats of Engineer Brotherhoods or Knights
of Labor to play havoc with all our means of

transportation, for they could survive without them, provided, of course, that a sufficient stock of tobacco had been laid in. And yet, with all their phlegm and apparent indifference to the outside world, they arose as one man when the news reached them of the first symptoms of a revolt against unjust taxation at Boston in 1774, and sent to that city their message of sympathy. Whatever may be true of other portions of the country, it seems conclusive that among the farmers along the Hudson and Hackensack there was from the first, practical unanimity in resisting this system of robbery, not only in council, but in arms, while at the same time, as in this instance of the address of the Bergen people, they were still loyal to the King. It was only when a part of the community thought that the object of the war might be accomplished without independence, and the other part differed with them, that there were deadly enemies in the same town, sometimes in the same house, and even in the same bed.

It was about three miles from Tappan when we passed the spot of one of the most bloody massacres of the war. It was where the American Col. Baylor had quartered himself and 116 men at the home and on the premises of Cornelius Haring, when some of Haring's Tory neighbors gave notice to the British over the river. Col. Grey accordingly, piloted by them, after crossing the Hudson, came upon the detachment unawares by night, and to the great delight of the Tories, massacred every one who could not make his escape.

Riding a few miles further down, after passing through Schraalenberg, we came near to the scene of the affray above Bull's Ferry, which, although serious and resulting in considerable loss of life on both sides, is remembered more for the comic description given of it by Major André in his poem entitled the "Cow Chace," in which he unmercifully ridiculed Gen. Wayne. Wayne's main object was to dislodge a force of Tories who had entrenched themselves in a block-house, and he also desired to get possession of a lot of cattle for the commissariat. André in his long string of verses puts this in the mouth of Wayne as issuing his orders to his subordinates:

> " I, under cover of th' attack,
>   Whilst you are all at blows,
>   From " English neighborhood " and Tamack
>   Will drive away the cows."

There is one stanza in this poem in which he writes of cold-blooded murder in such a rollicking style that unless, as it is charity to hope, he did not know what the circumstances were, our sympathy for the fate which befell him afterwards, might be entirely withdrawn, and men might say that his own request to "die without a rope" was denied him as a punishment for the utterance :

> "But, oh Thaddeus Possett, why
>   Should thy poor soul elope,
> And why should Titus Hooper die,
>   Ah, die—without a rope!"

Mr. Clayton says that Hooper "was murdered by the Tories under John Van de Roder, a neighbor, who entered his home in the night, and after shooting him through the head compelled his wife to hold a candle while they thrust nineteen bayonets into him."

What had Hooper done? Perhaps somebody can tell us something that may be said in extenuation of the brutal conduct of Van de Roder, and of the inhuman rhyme of André. The closing lines are almost prophetic of retribution :

" And now I close my epic verse ;
    I tremble as I show it,
Lest this same warrior-drover, Wayne,
    Should ever catch the poet. "

Musing on all these things, for though I had
not travelled many miles in the last two days,
I had travelled back many years, I gave
Fanny a loose rein and became careless of my
road.   She did not pay proper attention to the
sign-boards, but wandered off to the right
through some by-road of the undiscovered
country.   I think it was with instinct that she
might find a stopping-place for our midday
meal, for soon a little out-of-the-way Dutch
tavern hove in sight.   Why it was there I cannot tell.   There was no neighborhood of
houses whose tenants might frequent its bar-
room at evening, and all the custom that could
come to its doors must be that of the prudent
farmers going in and coming out from market,
men who are chary of the proceeds of their
cabbages and potatoes.

It must have been, as I have been, living on
the memories of the past.   Before it was a
wide stoop, and as I pulled up alongside, I
could see the portly landlord sitting in his
own company by the bar-room stove, quietly

smoking his pipe. He slowly turned his head, but made no effort to rise and open the door. I dismounted and entering the house, said, "Good afternoon." The landlord replied, "Goede namiddag." "Can I have my horse fed?" I asked. Whereupon he called out, "Hannes! Draag zorg of het paard dezer heer."

The boy came forth from another room, and led Fanny to the stable as I followed.

"Now," said I, after I had taken off the saddle and bridle, a proceeding rather above his comprehension, "give her four quarts of oats." "Wy hebben geen haver," replied the boy, shaking his head solemnly, by which I understood that there were no oats.

"What do you feed your own horses on, then?" I asked, as I surveyed two melancholy looking skeletons staggering about the barn-yard.

"Wy geven onzen paarden hooi," he answered.

Looking in the crib, I saw some Hackensack bulrushes, and I told the boy that my mare would not eat such stuff.

"Laat haar blyven voor een week Zy will honger genoeg hebben om it te eeten," said he.

After all, Dutch is not so very much unlike
English. It was easy enough to understand
this: "Let her stay a week and she will be
hungry enough to eat it." Perhaps she might,
but it was not more than twelve miles to New
York, so that Fanny was not compelled to try
the often-told experiment of the Irishman's
horse of living without eating, of which his
owner remarked that it was an entire success,
but that unfortunately "just as he got cliverly
larnt he died." I pitied her, but reminded
her of the old song which runs:

> " There was a man who had a cow;
>   He had no hay to give her.
>   He took his pipe and played the tune,
>   'Consider, cow, consider.'"

I gave her a lump of sugar, and promised to
bring her out a piece of bread to "stay her
stomach." The landlord could wrestle somewhat better with English than the boy, but
his language was very composite in its connection. He readily assented to my request
for some dinner, but when I ventured to ask
for a broiled chicken, having seen some fowls
picking about the premises, he awoke from his
stupor, and the blood coursed rapidly through

his veins. " Kip? Myn God ! " he exclaimed.
" Wat meant you? Neen, neen ! If I kill een
kip, de kip don't never be a hen, en daar won't
be no eyeren. If I killed kippen last year, you
don't won't get no eyeren mit your ham to-
day !" As the French say, " he had reason."
It was a sound argument, and I was convinced
of its force when a very nice dish of ham and
eggs was served by the vrouw of my landlord.
She was a woman with a head such as Rubens
was wont to paint, hair combed back and surmounted by a cap that might serve for day or
night; blue eyes, rosy cheeks and lips. She
was dressed in a short woollen gown with a
white apron in front and nothing behind ; she
could sit down without inconvenience to herself, and she could stand up in a crowd without
inconvenience to others.

Two little girls, with their yellow hair braided
and coiled on the backs of their heads, and
held in place by high horn combs, were sitting
on the floor, holding and balling up a skein of
yarn, and that uncarpeted floor was as clean as
the table-cloth and the bright ware upon it.
Surrounded by these pretty pictures, which
seemed to have been taken from their frames
and spread about for my entertainment, I dined

most agreeably ; and I may add that the feast
was moistened with a glass of choice Holland
gin, which the landlord informed me that he
did not sell, but sometimes gave to himself.
Poor Fanny had in the meantime employed
herself in pulling the sedge from the crib, and
trampling it under her feet in disgust. It was
her worst experience upon the journey.

The warm afternoon sun had played havoc
with the "beautiful snow," turning it into yellow water, which choked the gutters and overflowed the roads, and when we reached the
main thoroughfare all was slush and mud.
Wading through it, we came to the toll-bridge
over the Hackensack, and then to another toll-
gate at the causeway turnpike, and so on to
a Jersey driveway in feeble imitation of New
York avenues, with like shingle road-houses
and rows of sheds. We were no longer in the
country, but among unpaved and unmacada-
mized streets lined with saloons and breweries.
Huge lager-beer wagons, drawn by elephantine
horses and driven by animated beer casks,
splashed along. Then we came to the taper-
ing backbone of the Palisade range, which
finally loses itself at Hoboken, and, crossing

it, descended at Weehawken amid excavations, mud, filth, and wet coal dust, over a gridiron of railway tracks, to the "old ferry," which took us to New York.